'Tonight, let's
murmured

Then Nora rose up
mouth to his.

Pete's reaction was instant and intense. With
a low moan, he pressed her back against the door,
covering her mouth with his and pinning her
wrists above her head.

He wasn't going to be sorry for this in the
morning and neither would she—he'd make sure
of that.

Slowly, deliciously, he seduced her with his
tongue, moving from her mouth, to her neck,
to the warm valley between her breasts. With
insistent fingers, he tugged at her dress until the
pink tip of her breast was revealed. He gazed at
her with a hunger he'd never known, even as he
told himself that she would probably soon put an
end to this intimate adventure. Still…

Nora's breath caught as he drew her nipple into
his mouth, but rather than pull away, she melted
into him, making him forget everything but the
need to be deep inside her.

'How much further are you going to let this go?'
he asked, his voice thick with desire. 'Because if
we continue, I can't guarantee I'll be able to stop.'

She looked up at him brazenly. 'But what if I
don't want you to stop?'

Dear Reader,

It was a long time coming, but here it is—my first Blaze for Sensual Romance™. Those of you who read my books regularly will be a little surprised, I'm sure. After all, I'm more known for writing humour than hot, steamy sex. But when my editor challenged me to try my hand at a Blaze, I couldn't resist coming up with a story that was *very* sexy in both premise *and* execution. But nobody told me I couldn't make it funny as well…

First thing, I needed a good recipe for this spicy treat. So I started with Nora Pierce, a *very* frustrated etiquette columnist who's afraid she's losing her sensuality to her alter ego, prissy Prudence Trueheart. Then I added sexy sports writer, Pete Beckett, a guy who has a way with women—and a way of showing up in every one of Nora's private fantasies.

After I stirred in several other ingredients, such as secret identities and a one-night stand that turned into so many more, I came up with a story that I hope all of you will find sinfully delicious.

Enjoy,

Kate Hoffmann

ALL THROUGH THE NIGHT

by

Kate Hoffmann

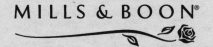

MILLS & BOON®

To my editor Brenda Chin, who believes in me
even when I don't. You're the best.

*First published in Great Britain 2001
by Harlequin Mills & Boon Limited,
Eton House, 18-24 Paradise Road, Richmond, Surrey TW9 1SR*

© Peggy A Hoffmann 2000

ISBN 0 263 82804 2

21-0601

*Printed and bound in Spain
by Litografia Rosés S.A., Barcelona*

1

THERE WASN'T MUCH he liked about Prudence True-heart. But he had to admit, he liked the way she moved.

Pete Beckett braced his arms along a low cubicle wall on the far side of the Bullpen, resting his chin on his hands. All around him, the employees of the *Herald*'s sports department rushed to make the noon deadline, frantically typing copy on computer terminals, the click of keys creating a familiar din. As a syndicated columnist, Pete met earlier deadlines, and his column was already out on the wire. And since he hadn't decided on tomorrow's subject, he found himself with nothing to do except ruminate on the physical attributes of the *Herald*'s uptight little etiquette columnist, Prudence Trueheart.

Though she always dressed in a tidy little suit and a prissy white blouse, starched board stiff, the body beneath the suit refused to comply with the outward image. To match the clothes, one might expect a ramrod-straight spine and a clipped gait, heels clicking on the floor, mouth pinched in a permanent expression of disapproval.

But the assumption would not be correct. Prudence possessed a fluid grace, her hips swaying ever so slightly with each step, her neck arched and her chin tipped up in subtle defiance. Her arms swung gracefully at her sides and her long fingers were delicately tipped in a conservative shade of cotton-candy pink.

And her mouth. Well, there was something about that mouth that made words of admonishment a waste of a pair of perfectly tempting lips. No matter how hard she tried to look like a Sunday School teacher, Pete couldn't get past the urge to pull every last bobby pin from the knot of pale hair at her nape. Or maybe yank her into his arms and kiss her senseless. Or at least suck on a few of those pretty fingertips.

"Giving Prudence the evil eye will not get you that corner office."

Pete turned to find Sam Kiley standing beside him, his gaze fixed on the same target. "Do you ever wonder what she's like outside the office?" Pete asked. "I mean, does she wear those suits to bed? And is that little bun on the back of her head a permanent thing, or does she let her hair loose when she walks in the front door of her house?"

Prudence disappeared into her office, and Pete craned his neck to see inside the open door. He just couldn't figure the contradiction. How could a woman with so much sensual presence, such an abundance of feminine appeal, be such a royal pain in the butt? This question had been bothering Pete for a long time, and though it begged an answer, he wasn't about to get close enough to the prickly Prudence to find out what that answer was.

"If you're really that curious, I suppose I could ask Ellie," Sam offered.

Ellie, the former Ellen Wilson, happened to be Sam Kiley's wife and the circulation manager for the *Herald*. She was also, coincidentally, Prudence Trueheart's best friend. Ellie and Sam had met at the paper and married just a year ago.

"I'm not curious," Pete lied, pushing back from the cubicle. He laughed dryly. "Why would I be curious about Prudence Trueheart?"

"She has a real name, you know," Sam said.

"Pierce," Pete murmured. "Laura—or is it Nora? Or maybe it's Nola. We've had a few conversations over the years. Once when I took her parking space, and another time when she accused me of stealing her stapler. I even kissed her once at a Christmas party. And I think I'm the only one in the sports department who reads her little memos. At least, before I rip them off the refrigerator door."

He couldn't really blame Prudence. As the *San Francisco Herald*'s only other syndicated columnist, she really didn't fit into any of the other departments at the paper. Prudence was an orphan of sorts and had been given the only available office commensurate with her salary and her value to the *Herald*. That office just happened to be in the sports department, though both she and Pete were coveting a huge corner office about to be vacated on the other end of the floor.

Hell, she might have had more luck with her memos in Lifestyles. Or even at the city desk. But trying to whip a bunch of rowdy sportswriters and footloose photographers into a polite group of co-workers was a near impossible task. Still, she never stopped trying. Every month, she posted a new memo about office etiquette in the lunchroom; from refrigerator hygiene to coffeepot protocol, there wasn't a rule of polite society that Prudence Trueheart didn't try to enforce.

But the Bullpen was called the Bullpen for a good

reason. And it wasn't populated solely by bullheaded men. The sportswriters and photographers at the *Herald*, male and female, were an odd lot, stubborn and single-minded in their love of any and all sports—and in their distaste for common courtesy. To some outsiders, they might seem like a bunch of arrested adolescents. But Pete liked the laid-back atmosphere and the daily games that began the moment the noon deadlines had passed. They worked hard and they played even harder.

He pushed aside thoughts of Prudence Trueheart, chiding himself for bothering to waste brain cells on her, then turned his attention to today's competition. On Thursday, they always played baseball. Other days it was hockey or golf or basketball. The diamond was laid out among the desks in the Bullpen, and a plastic ball and bat made the competition safe for windows and other breakable objects. Today, the competition would be against Sam Kiley and his motley crew of city beat reporters, easy marks for the money that was often wagered.

Glancing at the clock, Pete headed for the lunchroom to retrieve the ball and bat from a closet. As he grabbed the equipment, he glanced over at the refrigerator. A new note on crisp *Herald* stationery had been posted in Prudence's precise style. He stepped over and scanned the text. "'Property Rights for Food Owners,'" he muttered. Apparently, Prudence had had some yogurt that had gone missing a few days back.

Pete grabbed the paper and crumpled it in his fist. "Bottom of the ninth, game seven of the series. The bases are loaded and the winning run is at the plate. Beckett steps up into the batter's box and the crowd goes wild.'' He tossed the paper wad up into the air, then swung the bat. Prudence's memo went sailing across the room, hit the wall, then dropped into a wastebasket.

"Grand slam home run!" Pete held up his arms and bowed before walking out of the room. By the time he reached the Bullpen, the teams had assembled and were eagerly awaiting the start of the game. He tossed the ball at Sam Kiley and stepped into the batter's box. "Loser buys the beers at Vic's tomorrow afternoon," he called.

Kiley let the first pitch fly, low and away, and Pete took a swing, connecting with the whiffle ball and sending a line drive across the Bullpen—and right into the open door of Prudence Trueheart's office. An instant later a scream split the air, and Pete dropped the bat. The guys looked at each other and then at Pete.

He winced. "Hey, I didn't do it on purpose. That was a perfect line drive to right field. Ramirez didn't make the catch." He pointed at the sheepish sports photographer. "Error," he muttered.

Sam held up his hands in mock surrender. "You hit it, Beckett. You're the one who'll have to apologize."

Pete cursed softly. The last thing he needed was to be verbally dressed down by Prudence Trueheart, especially when he'd so recently fantasized about her mouth. Maybe if he just ignored his *faux pas*, she'd write another memo. But then, they only had one whiffle ball, and the game couldn't continue unless he ventured inside her office to retrieve it.

"I'll go," he finally said. He felt the same way he had as a kid, when Sister Amalia, his Catholic school principal, called him in to her office after he'd sent yet another wild pitch through the rectory window. "If I'm not out in five minutes, send a rescue party."

He crossed the Bullpen and slowly approached the office door. When he peeked inside, Pete expected to find a glowering Prudence, pacing her office like a hungry tiger, ready to tear him to shreds. Instead, he found her sitting on the floor next to her desk, rubbing her left brow. He quickly bent down and touched her ankle. "Are you all right?"

She looked up through watery blue eyes and blinked. The moment her gaze met his, Pete's lungs slowly ceased to function and breathing became impossible. He'd spent a fair amount of time speculating about the woman who occupied this office, but with her hair mussed and her glasses removed, he had to admit that she was much prettier at close range. Her complexion was flawless, her profile nearly perfect. Her full lips were parted slightly and her breathing shallow. She had a mouth made to be kissed, and kissed deeply—and had she been any other woman, Pete might have given it a try at that very moment.

Instead, he swallowed hard. "Nora," he murmured, his gaze dropping to her long, shapely legs and her trim ankles. Her name was Nora Pierce. He'd always thought of her as Prudence Trueheart, but now, with the scent of her perfume wafting through the air and the heat of her skin beneath his palm, she didn't seem much like a Prudence anymore.

Clearing her throat, she fixed her eyes on the spot where his hand rested on her leg, where his thumb idly stroked the inside of her ankle. Her gaze narrowed, and she picked up the plastic baseball and held it out. "Mr. Beckett. I believe this is yours."

Pete forced a smile. He snatched his hand away

from her ankle, then took the ball from her fingers, feeling as if he'd just stuck his hand beneath Sister Amalia's habit. "Thanks."

Her eyebrow rose every so slightly, disdainfully. "And?"

"And?" His mind raced. And what? Thank you *very much?* Was that what she was waiting for, some kind of superlative? He scowled, then glanced from the baseball to her cool glare—and the faint bruise growing beneath her eye. "Oh. *And.* And I apologize," he ventured. "I'm sorry. Truly sorry."

Her expression softened slightly, and he bit back a massive sigh of relief. "Thank you," she said. "Apology accepted. And maybe next time you could close my door before you begin your game?"

"Um," he murmured, letting his gaze drift over her body, taking in the buttons of her suit. They looked as if he could undo them in just a few seconds. Somewhere beneath that drab fabric was a woman's body, and from what he could see, it didn't deserve to be trussed up in such a conservative outfit. Pete clenched his fists and pushed the idea aside, returning his gaze to her face.

Nora rubbed her eye, then sucked in a sharp breath. As she tried to stand, he gently pushed her back down. "Here," he said, carefully pulling her fingers back. "Let me look at it."

"Am I bleeding?"

He stared into her eyes, such incredibly blue eyes. Why had he never noticed her eyes before? Wide and innocent eyes. Tantalizing. Alluring. A host of adjectives tumbled through his mind. A man could lose himself in those eyes. For a moment, he couldn't concentrate on anything else but the way her lashes fluttered, the way her honey-blond hair fell across her forehead; the soft pulse point just below her jaw that would feel so warm beneath his lips. She cleared her throat again, yanking him back to reality once more.

"No, you're not bleeding," he said. "It's not so bad. Just a little black and blue. You can hardly see it."

"Black and blue?" Nora moaned. "That can't be."

He shrugged, then stared at it more closely, probing at the bruise with a gentle touch. "You can put some of that makeup stuff on it, and no one will notice."

"But—but I can't have a black eye!"

A sharp laugh slipped from his throat before he could stop it. "Why? Do you have some hot date tonight?" When he saw the flush of embarrassment creep up her cheeks, he cursed himself soundly. "I'm sorry. I shouldn't have laughed."

"No, you shouldn't have," she murmured. "It was very rude."

"I just never think of you...I mean, Prudence... Well, you know what I mean. I never think of Prudence as having much of a social life, beyond quilting bees and pinochle club."

"I'm not Prudence," she said in a soft voice, the hurt evident beneath the surface. "And—and maybe I do have a date tonight. Would that be so hard to believe?"

He let his palm rest on her cheek for a moment before he sat back on his heels. "Well, you're going to have a nice shiner, Nora Pierce, if you don't put some ice on that eye." Pete reached out and took her hand, then helped her to her feet. "I'll get something from the fridge. Why don't you sit down? And don't rub it. I'll be right back."

Nora nodded and managed a grateful smile, as he

strode out of her office. The boys were gathered in a small group, ready to mount a rescue mission. But he waved as he passed, tossing them the ball. "She's fine," he said. "Carry on. I'm going to get some ice. I hit her in the eye."

Fear froze the expressions of his co-workers, and they quickly scattered, heading back to work before they might be implicated in the injury of Prudence Trueheart. Pete grabbed the closest thing he could find to an ice pack from the refrigerator and hurried back to Nora's office.

He found her leaning back in her chair, her eyes closed and her slender legs stretched out in front of her, crossed at the ankles.

"Here," he murmured, bending over her, bracing his hand on the arm of her chair. "This should help."

Nora opened her eyes and looked at the small package he offered. "That's a frozen burrito."

Pete shrugged. "Someone forgot to fill the ice trays."

She took the burrito from his hand and carefully placed it over her eye. "Another breach of office etiquette—actually, two. Stolen food and empty ice trays."

He covered her hand with his and adjusted the burrito over the bruise. An errant strand of hair slipped from the knot at her nape and brushed the back of his hand. He was acutely aware of how soft it felt. It probably smelled good, too. "Yeah, I guess that memo you put up must have fallen off the refrigerator already."

"You tore it down, didn't you," Nora accused.

"Not me," he lied. "But you have to admit, sometimes you are a little..."

"Pushy?" she asked. "Overbearing?"

"I was going to say 'prissy,'" he replied, stepping back before he was tempted to run his fingers through her hair and scatter the pins that held it in place. Actually, he was going to say "autocratic and oppressive." But the vulnerability he saw in her eyes made him amend his opinion. Suddenly, he much preferred Nora Pierce's gratitude to her disapproval. "Sports guys don't like rules. The only thing that should have rules is a game."

"Civilized society needs proper etiquette," she countered. "If we have to live together, we have to respect each other. Good etiquette is a measure of that respect."

"And twenty-seven rules posted on an office refrigerator tend to make us a little crazy."

She sighed softly, tipping her head back and closing her eyes. "I don't mean to make you crazy. I was just trying to be...helpful."

His attention dropped to her mouth again, and he fought the impulse to lean closer and kiss away the traces of hurt he heard in her voice. He'd always assumed she was such a hard and calculating woman, an imperious force with a steel spine and ice water running through her veins. But in truth, Nora Pierce wasn't at all like Prudence Trueheart. Sure, she was a little uptight and overly concerned with propriety. But beneath the stuffy facade, she was soft and vulnerable and incredibly irresistible.

"Maybe I could take you out to lunch," he said. "By way of an apology."

She sat up straight and pulled the burrito from her eye, regarding him with a suspicious expression. "Lunch?"

"Yeah, why not? That's not against the rules, is it?

Or didn't I ask the right way. Should I have called first? Or maybe written you a note? I suppose I could have sent an engraved invitation, but my engraver is broken."

Nora shook her head, the barest hint of a smile touching her lips. "I—I don't think lunch would be such a good idea. After all, we work together. People might talk."

Though it was a reputation built more on rumor than fact, Pete was known at the *Herald* as the resident Casanova, a fact that obviously hadn't escaped Prudence's notice. He didn't put much effort into attracting women, but he always seemed to have at least two or three beautiful ladies on a string. Yet, over the past year, he'd found himself increasingly disenchanted with the women he dated—and the reputation he'd cultivated. Unfortunately, the reputation seemed to stick, and his personal life had become tasty fodder for the office gossips.

It wasn't that he didn't like women anymore. He still had the occasional date, but maybe he was getting too old for the singles scene. At thirty-three, he wasn't exactly over the hill, but he'd come to the conclusion that a good relationship wasn't only about great sex and a centerfold body. He just wasn't sure what it *was* about.

Pete sighed. At the moment, he found himself wanting lunch with Nora Pierce, odd as that seemed. "It's just a simple lunch," he said with a grin. "What could they possibly say about you and me having a burger together?" Though he meant the question rhetorically, he saw another trace of hurt in her expression, then realized how she'd taken it. Of course, a quiet lunch with Prudence Trueheart couldn't possibly end in anything other than dessert and separate checks. She had her reputation, too, and it was spotless. But her reaction came out of left field, and he wasn't sure if he should apologize or rephrase.

"I—I'm not hungry, but thank you, anyway," Nora replied, her voice suddenly cold and distant. She held out the burrito. "Here, you better put this back in the freezer. I wouldn't want anyone to miss it."

Pete slowly shook his head and took the burrito. For a few minutes, he'd thought he'd managed a truce of sorts with Nora Pierce—maybe even the beginning of a friendship. But after sticking his foot in his mouth, not once but twice, he realized that the woman before him would be a tough sell. If discarding his reputation meant losing his touch with women, maybe he'd have to rethink his options.

"Fine," he murmured. "But if you change your mind, just let me know." He walked to the door, then turned around to take one last look. She watched him from behind her desk, her blue eyes wide. He should have insisted on lunch, or at least been insulted by her refusal. But something told him not to burn any more bridges with Nora. "I'll...see you later."

She nodded curtly, then picked up a file folder from her desk and efficiently spread the contents out in front of her. When she'd managed to ignore him for a full ten seconds, he silently walked out of her office, closing the door behind him.

The teams had reassembled in the Bullpen, and the game had started up again with Sam Kiley's team at bat. As he walked back to his spot in the infield, he caught a foul ball and threw it to the first baseman.

"So? What happened?" Sam asked.

"The hell if I know," Pete murmured. "I'm usually

pretty good at figuring out women, but Prudence Trueheart is one confusing lady." He took his place as shortstop, rubbing his palms on his thighs. His mind drifted back to the feel of her skin beneath his fingertips. It wasn't going to be so easy to write off Prudence Trueheart—or Nora Pierce, for that matter. Besides confusing and capricious and condescending, he found her incredibly intriguing.

And it had been such a long time since Pete Beckett had found any woman intriguing.

Dear Prudence Trueheart,
My boyfriend and I have been doing the nasty from the night of our first date. The sex is fantastic, but now that our wedding date is approaching, I'd like to practice celibacy to make the wedding night special. How can I convince my horny fiancé of my decision?
Signed, Steadfast in San José

Nora Pierce read the letter over again and again, crossing out the word *horny* and replacing it with *ardent,* then trying to come up with a euphemism for *the nasty.* But the edit couldn't possibly change the tone of the letter. This wasn't etiquette! This was a country-and-western song. A bad talk show topic. Beauty parlor gossip. She sighed and rubbed her forehead. When she'd taken the job as Prudence three years ago, she'd been hired to answer questions about gracious living. But all that had changed on April Fool's Day six months ago.

On a lark, she'd answered a silly question from a cross-dresser who wanted to know whether he should ask his wife's permission first before borrowing her underwear or whether the lingerie was community property. Her answer dripped with sarcasm and disapproval, and she'd published it to illustrate the limits of true etiquette. "The only excuse a man has for not wearing proper underwear is if he's not wearing any underwear at all!" she'd written. "And the only places where underwear can be considered an option is in the shower and the doctor's office."

That single, silly column had been the end of her noble life as an etiquette columnist. The phone lines lit up and the fan mail poured in to all the newspapers across the country that carried her column. Her readers wanted more—more dirt, more trash, more sleaze. And more of Prudence's sharp-tongued reprimands and subtle put-downs.

"Great column yesterday!"

Nora glanced up. Her publisher, Arthur Sterling, leaned into the doorway of her office, a broad smile on his face. Though he rarely descended from the twelfth floor, he'd been seen more often lately in Prudence's vicinity. Though a more naive columnist might believe they'd become friends, Nora knew that Arthur Sterling had no friends. He had assets and opportunities. And he wanted her to agree to syndicated television spots as "Prudence."

He chuckled and nodded his head. "Sex, that's what sells. I just got off the phone with Seattle. They want the column. And Biloxi and Buffalo are in negotiations as we speak." Arthur gave her the thumbs-up. "Good work! And I'm still waiting for your answer on that television deal."

"Thank you," she murmured. But he was already gone, on to some other profit center, some other opportunity that was going to pad his already sizable bank account. To him, Prudence wasn't a beacon in a sea of chaos, a behavioral standard. She'd become dollars and cents. More trash meant more readers. And that meant more money for her syndicated column. Etiquette is part of the past, he'd told her. It might have been all right for the first Prudence Trueheart in 1921, but the world was changing.

If only she'd never written that April Fool's column. Since then, Sterling had insisted she devote at least three columns a week to "modern" problems—questions on morality and relationships. Her monthly appearance on *Good Morning, San Francisco*, a popular television show, had turned from table settings and wedding etiquette to advice for the lovelorn.

With her sudden rise to popularity, she had become a celebrity around town. For every moment that Nora felt as if she were prying into her readers' personal lives, her readers seemed to intrude on hers. The grocery store, the dry cleaners, even the dentist's office—all had become venues for advice sessions. And her readers seemed to cherish Prudence's impeccable behavior even more than she did, always watching her, waiting to catch her in a manners misstep or a moral backslide! Prudence was supposed to be pure of heart and filled with virtue.

To ensure the purity of Prudence, her publisher had even included a morals clause in her contract. Prudence didn't curse or chew tobacco. She didn't wear revealing clothes or frequent biker bars. And she certainly didn't sleep around! That final point hadn't taken much effort on her part. She could barely remember the last time she'd been with a man, in the biblical sense.

Nora groaned and buried her face in her hands,

shaking her head. Her lack of contact with the opposite sex had become painfully obvious in her unbidden reaction to Pete Beckett's touch. And since she'd been beaned by that baseball, she'd been having a difficult time keeping her mind on work, preferring, instead, to dwell on the color of Pete Beckett's eyes and the warmth of his smile.

She thought back to their conversation, to her disturbing reaction to his touch, to the feel of his gaze on her body. She replayed the incident, trying to remember every detail and every word spoken. "'Prissy,'" she murmured. Is that really what he thought of her?

She silently scolded herself and snatched up another letter. Nora had always found a certain comfort in Prudence's world, a place where there were rules and obligations, where people behaved with propriety and decorum. And where scoundrels and rogues like Pete Beckett saw the error of their ways, settled down with one woman, and lived blissfully ever after in legal and loyal matrimony.

But Prudence wasn't going to hold her breath on that front. The paper's golden boy, Beckett, was charming and handsome and a confirmed reprobate. He was everything Prudence Trueheart preached against: a man practiced in the art of seduction and an expert in avoiding commitment, the typical bad boy that Prudence found so troubling—and other women found so irresistible.

Though she never deliberately listened to office gossip, what she did overhear was probably mere speculation. Or pure exaggeration. But from the soft moans and furtive giggles from the female members of the staff, she had to believe that some of what she'd overheard was true—enough to spend a small portion of each day wondering just what Pete Beckett did to a woman once he got her behind the bedroom door. Not that she'd ever find out. When they did bother to communicate, Nora regarded Pete Beckett with thinly disguised disdain, and Pete regarded Nora with mocking amusement.

Still, it wasn't hard to imagine the power he could wield over women, considering her own reaction to his touch. He had beautiful hands, long fingers and a firm, but gentle, touch. A shiver skittered down her spine, and she thought about how those hands would look as they slowly undressed her, how they might feel on her flushed skin, all the improper things he might do to her body, given the chance.

She brushed her thumb over her bottom lip. This wasn't the first physical contact they'd shared, she mused. He'd kissed her once, at the *Herald*'s Christmas party, right after she'd been promoted to the job as "Prudence." Though he probably didn't remember, a vivid image flashed in her mind...standing beneath the mistletoe, the feel of his hard mouth on hers, the gentle teasing of his tongue, and that exquisite and unbidden longing deep in her core.

It had happened so quickly, she couldn't protest, but once Nora was caught up in the kiss, she recalled abandoning all resistance, defenseless beneath his touch. When he finally let her go, he gave her a teasing smile and made some comment about old maids and untried virgins before he moved on to other amusements. She'd gotten a lot of mileage out of that kiss in those moments when she was curled up in a lonely bed, when sleep just wouldn't come.

Now she had another real-life encounter to add to her fantasies. She thought back to the instant that his hand had touched her ankle, to the warmth of his fingers sinking into her skin, the first physical contact from a man in oh-so long. She recalled the way he touched her face, his breath warm against her temple, the scent of his cologne so heady and—

Nora cursed softly. How did they do it? How did all those bad boys make good women lose all common sense? She'd railed at her readers time and time again, and yet, here she was, falling into the same trap, forgiving the man all his sins for just a simple touch of his hand, a brush of his lips against hers. She reached for her keyboard, her indignation rising with the spirit of all Prudences past.

Dearest Reader,
You opened the stable door on your first date and now it's going to be difficult to herd that stallion back inside. Prudence believes you should stand firm in your decision. Celibacy is a virtue and your body a prize to be treasured. If this man can't respect your feelings, then send him straight to the glue factory. And please, promise Prudence that you won't go riding again until you've said "I do."

The horse metaphor was a little trite, yet it was typical Prudence—smart, sassy, with just a touch of sarcasm. Nora reached out and typed in the command that would send her column to her copy editor. Though times had changed, the words could just as easily have belonged to the very first Prudence, a woman named Hortense Philpot who rode herd on etiquette problems in the roaring twenties.

Nora had been hired as an assistant by Prudence IV,

right out of Stanford. With an undergraduate degree in medieval art, her job prospects had been slim. But she'd possessed something more valuable than a degree: a pedigree from a socially prominent San Francisco family that gave her a genetic predisposition to proper etiquette. She'd been born and raised in Sea Cliff, the bastion of social propriety.

Upon Prudence IV's retirement, Nora had signed a five-year contract as the new Prudence. She'd taken the job because—well, because there wasn't much call in San Francisco for an expert in medieval tapestries. But she also thought she might be able to inject a little class and propriety into the everyday life of her readers.

She pulled off her horn-rimmed glasses and rubbed her eyes, then reached for the stack of letters her assistant had selected for upcoming columns. Pushing up from her chair, she began to pace the office. "Infidelity," she murmured, tossing the first letter onto the floor. "Deception." As she flipped through the letters, she found new problems to replace the old problems she'd just solved. "Anger. Resentment. Dysfunctional families. Sexual fantasies."

Nora stood and wandered by the window that overlooked the Bullpen. She peeked through the slats of the miniblinds. They were still playing their silly little game, and Pete Beckett was in the middle of it all. She watched as he stretched to catch the ball, his shirt pulled taut against his torso. Even from a distance, Nora could see the outline of his narrow waist and muscular chest. All thoughts of work slipped from her mind. "Sexual fantasies," she murmured.

All right, maybe she did find Pete Beckett incredibly attractive. But that was just a physical reaction. It had nothing to do with the man, just the body. A flat belly and a cute butt certainly didn't mitigate his bad qualities. Nor did chiseled features and a perfect profile...or his short-cropped dark hair, always so casually mussed, as if some woman had recently run her fingers through it. And maybe he did have a smile that was known to melt a girl's heart, but he rarely turned it on her. Nora had heard that women found his devilish sense of humor quite irresistible, though when he bothered to toss a tiny bit of his charm in her direction she usually reciprocated with some shrewish reply.

"Any juicy letters today?"

Nora jumped away from the window, the slats snapping back into place. Ellen Kiley stood in the doorway of her office. Embarrassed to be caught spying, Nora sent her friend a disapproving frown, then handed her a letter. "You, too? Have you joined those at the *Herald* who believe sleaze sells?"

Ellie had started at the *Herald* the very same day Nora had, and they'd been inseparable friends, at least until Ellie had married Sam Kiley a year ago. "I'm the circulation manager. When the circulation goes up, I'm happy. So what's got your knickers in a bundle, Prude?"

"Don't call me that!" Nora sighed, surprised by her reaction to Ellie's gentle teasing. She flopped down in her office chair and gazed up at her friend. "When you think of me, do you really think of me as Prudence Trueheart? Or as Nora Pierce?"

Ellie frowned and sat down across from her, her gaze fixed on the letter. "I don't get it," she murmured. "What's the difference?"

"There *is* a difference!" Nora cried, leaning over her desk and snatching the letter from her friend's hand.

"Don't you see?" She crumpled the paper and tossed it aside, then began to pace the width of her office. "I'm not Prudence Trueheart. I put words in her mouth, but she's not me. And I'm not her."

"Is something wrong?"

"Nothing's wrong," Nora said, unwilling to explain further. But she couldn't hold in her frustration any longer. "It's just that sometimes I get sick of Prudence. She's so...prissy!" Only after the word slipped from her lips did she realize it was Pete's word again, *his* description of her. "People expect me to be her. And it's getting awfully hard lately to figure out where she ends and I begin."

"A lot of people have trouble separating work from their personal life," Ellie offered.

"I—I just expected things to be different. When I first got a job at the *Herald*, I thought my life was going to change. I moved out of my parents' house, away from my mother, and I found that little apartment in the Castro. I expected my life to be more exciting. Look at me now. I dress in these suits and ride around on my high horse all day long, looking down my nose at ordinary mortals and scolding them for falling short of their moral and ethical duties." The last was said with a hysterical edge, and Nora took a deep breath to calm herself. "How can I advise people about passion when I have no passion in my life?"

The question caused Ellie to pause before answering. "You're very passionate about your work...about etiquette."

"A person can be passionate, but still have no passion in their life. Look at these letters." She picked up a stack and tossed it across the desk. "These people have passion. They live by their hearts, not their heads. I've never had that. Sure, there have been men in my life. Lovers, even. But I've never felt passion so overwhelming that it dissolves common sense. That it makes me crazy. And the longer I'm Prudence, the worse it gets."

Nora yanked open her desk drawer and pulled out a bag of peanut M&Ms. Shoving a handful into her mouth, she waited for the chocolate to soothe her. "I should just quit," she mumbled, her mouth full. Prudence never talked while she ate, but Nora was past caring about good manners. "I could go back to school. Get my doctorate in art history. Find a job in Paris or Rome."

"You can't quit. You're the heir apparent to both Dear Abby and Miss Manners. And you make more money than anyone at the *Herald*, except for maybe Pete Beckett. And someday, you're going to be a multimedia goddess, just like Martha Stewart."

"Don't say *that* name in *this* office," Nora said, popping another handful of candy into her mouth.

"Martha Stewart?"

"No, Pete Beckett. He is the antithesis of everything Prudence Trueheart values in a man. He's fickle and shallow and unscrupulous and—and because of him, I have this black eye!"

Ellie squinted to examine Nora's injury. "And how does Nora Pierce feel about him?" she asked pointedly.

Nora stopped cold, realization hitting her like a sharp slap to the face. She coughed slightly, an M&M lodged in her throat. "That—that is how I feel about him. The way he treats women is appalling. Promiscuity is a trait that both Prudence and I detest."

"Now you sound like your mother!"

Nora groaned.

"You also sound a little jealous," Ellie observed. "Just how much time do you spend thinking about Pete Beckett's romantic life?"

"None at all," Nora lied. She thought about evading the subject, but Ellie was her best friend, and they never held back anything from each other. "It just that after he hit me with the baseball, he—"

"He hit you with a baseball?"

"A whiffle ball. And it was an accident. He came into my office to apologize and he—he touched me. It was completely innocent, but I realized that I haven't been touched by a man—I mean, not in *that* way—for three whole years. Exactly the same amount of time that I've been Prudence Trueheart." She sighed. "I don't think I could attract a man if I danced naked on Nob Hill."

Ellie patted her on the shoulder. "That's not true. You're a very desirable woman! You could have any man you wanted, if you'd just put a little effort into it. When was the last time you went out?"

"Prudence Trueheart doesn't frequent singles bars," Nora said, her voice dripping with sarcasm.

"Well, maybe it's about time you got back into the swing of things," Ellie said.

"How?"

"I don't know," Ellie said with a shrug. "You're the advice columnist. Answer an ad, join a church group, take a class. Isn't that what you tell your readers?"

"That will take too long. I need immediate gratification."

Ellie gasped. "Don't you think you're taking this a little too fast?"

"Not *that* kind of gratification," Nora replied. "I just

need to know that I'm still attractive. That men find me alluring and intriguing."

"Well, that's easy, then. Tonight, you and I will go out. And we'll stay out until you meet a man. You'll flirt a little, maybe even kiss him. And if you really like him, you can give him your phone number."

Presented with a real plan, Nora suddenly wasn't sure she wanted to venture into such dangerous territory. What if she went out, and no one even bothered to look her way? "No man is going to want to date Prudence Trueheart."

"You don't have to tell him who you are. You could wear that disguise, that wig you bought a few months ago—the one you wear grocery shopping. You told me when you're in disguise, people don't recognize you."

Nora blinked, the simple perfection of Ellie's plan slowly sinking in. All the fun without any of the consequences. She could say and do whatever she wanted, become a completely different person if she wanted to. "I don't know," Nora said. "A disguise in this situation seems a little deceptive, don't you think?"

"You're going to flirt a little, not sell national secrets to the Russians. Who will you be hurting?"

Nora considered the plan for a moment. "I—I guess it could be like research. A little experiment. After all, if I'm expected to give advice, I should at least get out there and see what's going on, don't you think?" She looked up at Ellie expectantly. "So, are we on for tonight?"

Nora knew that if she gave herself even one more hour to think about this, she'd never go through with it. Her sense of propriety and good breeding would win out. It was time to stop thinking and rethinking every single aspect of her life. It was time to take action!

Ellie smiled and shook her head. "All right. Be dressed by eight."

"What should I wear?"

"Something provocative, of course. If you wear that suit, you'll be lucky if the bartender talks to you."

Suddenly, Nora wasn't sure action was the best plan. Maybe she should take some time to think about this. "I don't own anything provocative. And where would we go?"

"You've got the whole afternoon. Go buy yourself a new dress. And I'll ask Sam where we should go. He'll know a good place with lots of available men." She gave Nora a hug. "This is going to be so good for you."

With that, Ellie hurried out, leaving Nora standing in the middle of her office. Nora drew in a shaky breath, then let it out slowly. The only way she'd feel really good tomorrow morning was if she woke up with a man in her bed: a long-limbed, hard-muscled male with nothing on his mind but multiple orgasms—*her* multiple orgasms.

Though Nora was determined to throw off the Prudence Trueheart persona, she wasn't sure she could ever go that far. A one-night stand sounded so brazen, so impulsive, so far beyond anything she was capable of. She'd settle for something far less dangerous. Instead, she'd charm and bedazzle some stranger, perhaps even give him her phone number. She'd gather some real-life experience to pass on to her readers and

reassure herself that she was still an attractive and desirable woman.

And at the end of the night, maybe she would feel a
little more like Nora Pierce and a lot less like Prudence
Trueheart.

2

A HAZE OF CIGARETTE SMOKE hung over the noisy crowd at Vic's Sports Emporium, a popular watering hole near Fisherman's Wharf. The blare of big-screen televisions, all tuned to different sporting events, mixed with the chatter of voices and occasional cheers. Distractions were plentiful at Vic's. Even so, Pete noticed the woman the instant she walked in. Determined to keep his mind on the Giants' game, he wrote off his interest as an instinctive reaction born of so many years on the make.

But his eyes were inexplicably drawn back to her, a slender, raven-haired beauty in a form-fitting black dress. Maybe it was the way she moved, the subtle sway of her hips, the gentle arch of her neck, the oh-so-cool expression. Something about her captured his attention, and he couldn't help but stare. She didn't belong in Vic's, that much was certain. Vic's was a beer-and-pretzel kind of place, and this woman was champagne and caviar all the way.

The clues were nearly imperceptible, at least to anyone who didn't bother to look beneath the surface. But Pete had come across a lot of women in his dating days and he could tell real class when he saw it. Her dress—no doubt, designer labeled—fit her perfectly, hugging every curve of her body, yet coming nowhere near vulgar. It revealed only enough to tantalize: a glimpse of shoulder, a hint of cleavage, and just enough thigh to prove she had incredible legs beneath that skirt. No, she didn't need to advertise her assets. For this woman, a guy could certainly use his imagination.

But there was more—the way her gaze drifted around the room, never resting on one subject for long. She'd caused a minor stir as she made her way to the bar—men turning to watch her pass, jaws slack, eyes slightly glazed—yet she didn't notice her effect. Had her Mercedes broken down outside? Or had she somehow wandered out of a Nob Hill soiree and become lost in the fog? There wasn't a guy in the place who wouldn't give his right arm to help her. But they knew enough to keep their distance, not willing to risk an icy rebuff in front of friends.

Before she'd wandered in, Pete had been casually watching the ball game on one of the three televisions above the bar, nursing the same beer he'd bought during the first inning. It was only after she sat down at an empty spot midway down the bar that he realized she'd walked in with a companion, a woman he recognized instantly—Ellen Kiley! Pete grinned and picked up his beer. He hadn't come to Vic's to socialize, but maybe he'd consider changing his plans.

First, he was mildly curious why Ellie was out without Sam. Second, he thought it strange that Sam had never mentioned this beauty, never tried to set the two of them up. Maybe that was because Pete usually didn't go for the high-society type. But after spending the first half of the ball game bothered with thoughts of Nora Pierce, he needed something or someone to get his mind off the *Herald*'s uptight little etiquette columnist.

All night long, his thoughts had constantly wandered back to their encounter in her office earlier that afternoon. Pete had known a lot of women in his life, and they always fell into one of two categories: lovers who had become friends, and friends who had become lovers. He'd learned by experience that the two were mutually exclusive. A woman couldn't be both at the same time. Pete figured if he ever found a woman who could, he'd have to marry her.

But where did Nora Pierce fit in? She didn't want to be his friend. And she certainly had no interest in becoming his lover. Hell, he wasn't even sure she *liked* him! All he was really sure of was that, from the moment he had touched her, something had sparked between them, an attraction that was both irresistible and irrational. Every instinct he possessed told him to put Nora Pierce out of his head, but that was easier said than done.

Pete ordered another beer and watched Ellie from across the bar. He raised his hand to wave, but she quickly turned away, as if she hadn't seen him at all—or didn't want *him* to see *her*. Frowning, he grabbed his beer and slowly pushed away from the bar, determined to find out what she was up to. But as he neared the spot where they sat, she slipped off her bar stool and headed in the direction of the ladies' room. He nearly followed, but then decided to wait at the bar with Ellie's beautiful friend. After all, she couldn't stay in the ladies' room all night.

He put on his most charming smile, even though, in truth, he wished Ellie had walked in with Nora Pierce. Then he might have had a chance to talk to her outside the restrictive atmosphere of the office, to figure out this strange fascination he had with her, to melt her icy facade. He stood beside Ellie's stool and set his beer on the bar.

"Hi, there. Mind if I sit down?"

The woman gave him a brief glance, then coyly turned away, avoiding his gaze. The direct approach had always worked like a charm for him, but obviously not tonight. And not with this woman. Jeez, maybe he *was* losing his touch.

"My friend is sitting there," she said, her voice low and throaty. "She's gone to the ladies' room. She really won't be long."

She risked another quick look up at him, and it was then that he caught a whiff of her perfume, an exotic floral scent he recognized immediately. His mind raced to put a face to the scent, flipping through images of old lovers and even maiden aunts. But one face kept intruding, and it was only then that he realized he'd experienced the scent just that afternoon, when he'd touched Nora Pierce.

Pete leaned over the bar and caught a brief glimpse of her profile, proof positive that beneath the dark wig and artfully applied makeup, the lush red lipstick and kohl-rimmed eyes, lurked none other than Prudence Trueheart. He was tempted to blow her cover right off, but she was trying so hard to avoid detection that he decided to play along—at least for a little while.

So there was no Mercedes or Nob Hill party. Then, what had brought Prudence Trueheart to Vic's? Was she here to police bar etiquette, ready to shut the joint down for the lack of cloth napkins beneath the drinks and silver-plated toothpicks in the olives? Or had she come for the same reason other women came to Vic's—to meet men? *Prudence Trueheart on the make*, he mused. The night was about to get interesting.

"Can I buy you a drink?" he asked.

"May," she murmured, her voice cool. "May you buy me a drink. And, no, thank you, I have a drink." She picked up her club soda and took a delicate sip, then forced a smile. "My friend is coming right back."

"I'll just sit here until she does," Pete replied. Had she been any other woman, she might have blown him off with an acidic phrase or an arctic look. Instead, she gives him a grammar lesson. He grinned and slid onto the stool next to her. A gentleman might have taken the hint and retreated. But Pete Beckett wasn't going anywhere.

His gaze drifted along her body. The dress hugged every delicious curve, clinging to perfect breasts and a tiny waist, and making his palms itch to touch her again. There was only one reason Prudence Trueheart would slip into a slinky little number like that. She was out to seduce—or be seduced. And his appearance had just thrown a wrench into the works. Pete frowned. And what the hell was with the wig? He preferred her hair the way it was, pale gold and filled with light and framing her pretty features.

"I should go find my friend," she said in a breathless tone. She grabbed her purse and slid off her bar stool, but he reached out and took her wrist, stopping her escape. Her skin felt like warm silk beneath his fingers, the sensation of touching her again sending a flash of heat through his body so intense it made his head swim. He wondered what it might feel like to let his hands just wander, to make her breath quicken and her pulse race, to press his palms into the soft flesh of her breasts and to span her waist with both his hands. Already, the feel of her skin had been imprinted on his brain, and he craved more, like an addiction that wouldn't go away.

"Don't," he murmured. "Stay and have a drink with me. Just one drink."

He thought she'd refuse, but then she looked him squarely in the eyes and waited for what felt like a long moment. Neither of them said a word; they simply stared as if sizing each other up. And then she released a tightly held breath and resumed her spot next to him. She wasn't going to admit who she was, Pete realized. Prudence was going to go along with her little game, as long as he did. As far as she was concerned, they were complete strangers.

Pete had played more than his share of games with women, both in bed and out. Head games or bed games, he'd become quite adept at both. Then why did he feel so clueless now? Maybe because Nora Pierce didn't seem to be the type to engage in risky flirtations with strange men. But then, he wasn't a stranger, was he. Maybe he was just an available patsy, an unsuspecting dope who was about to get dumped, all for a tale that could be told over the office water cooler. This could all be payback for the black eye.

Pete cursed silently and raked his hand through his hair. Well, two could play at her little game. As long as it meant he could spend a few more minutes with her, he'd just play along. He motioned the bartender over. "Champagne," he said. "Your best."

Nora sent him a questioning look. "Champagne?"

"I'm having a drink with the most beautiful woman in this place. I think champagne is in order, don't you?"

Her gaze fixed on her wrist where his fingers still

rested. "There are a lot of beautiful women in this place," she said, pulling away.

Pete glanced around. "Yeah, I guess there are." The bartender popped the cork on a bottle of champagne and poured them both a glass. Pete picked up a flute and handed it to Nora. "But none more beautiful than you."

That brought a reluctant smile, as she took a sip of her champagne. "With a line like that line, maybe I should invest in champagne futures."

"Naw," Pete teased. "There wouldn't be much money in it. I gave up women a few months back."

She gave him a suspicious look, leveled at him over the rim or the champagne flute. "Then why are you bothering me?"

He reached out and ran a finger slowly down her bare arm. Maybe this little game wasn't so bad. At least it gave him free rein to touch her whenever he felt the urge. "Believe me, you're not a bother. In fact, you're the first woman in nearly a year who has made me regret my decision."

This time she laughed out loud, tipping her head back and letting loose with a musical giggle as bright as the bubbles that sparkled in her glass. In earlier days, he might have been insulted. But her delight captivated him, and he laughed along with her. Pete set his glass down, then braced his feet on her bar stool, his knees on either side of hers, trapping her in front of him.

Her giggle died in her throat as he stared into her eyes. He'd never wanted a woman as much as he wanted Nora Pierce. Not at that moment, not ever. But he knew he'd need to proceed cautiously, because behind the wide eyes and flushed features was a lady playing a dangerous game.

Gently, deliberately, he wove his fingers through hers, then pressed his lips to the back of her hand. "So, why don't we start with introductions?" he murmured, his words warm against her skin. "My name's Beckett. Pete Beckett. What's yours?"

He glanced up at her and sent her a charming grin. The game had begun, and he'd just upped the ante.

NORA TOOK A LONG GULP of her champagne, the bubbles tickling her nose and going right to her head. But no matter how muddled her mind became, one thought screamed from within. *Run away, run as fast and as far as you can from this man whose mouth is teasing at the inside of your wrist, whose words have the capacity to render you defenseless—this man who's demanded to know your name.*

Her big night out was supposed to be a simple experiment, a chance to dip her toe into the dating pool without risk of being swept away by the tide. But sitting here next to Pete, she felt as if the water were rushing up around her neck and the currents were threatening to pull her under. She wanted to blurt her name out to the entire bar—Nora Pierce or Prudence Trueheart, what did it matter? This little charade had to end!

But something held her back, a curiosity that needed to be satisfied, an undeniable magnetism that made all common sense vanish. Why not just see where the evening might lead, alter the experiment just a bit? She wasn't doing too badly. Except for her impromptu grammar lesson, she'd managed to hold her own in conversation without sounding too up-tight.

And it felt so good to stand in someone else's four-inch spike heels, to become the kind of woman she'd never been—sexy, provocative, irresistible. It wasn't that hard to step outside herself. Besides, she could walk away at any time, couldn't she? Nora stifled a long sigh. Perhaps that was easier said than done.

It wasn't the mental aspect of her charade that was so difficult, but the physical reactions she was having to endure. The shock of Pete Beckett turning up beside her had temporarily stolen the breath from her lungs. And then he'd touched her, and her heart had begun to somersault in her chest, beating a crazy rhythm. Every thought in her head became fixed on the mes-merizing way his fingers skimmed over her skin and warmed her blood. At once afraid and exhilarated, she had tried to keep one foot in reality, but she kept slip-ping into a realm that until now had been pure fan-tasy.

Why hadn't he recognized her? Could her disguise be that good? Earlier in the day they'd spoken, come face to face in her office. Surely she couldn't be that forgettable, could she? Nora brushed aside the notion. He'd had a few too many beers, that was it. Or maybe he hadn't yet noticed the faint bruise below her eye, barely concealed by her makeup. Or perhaps the thought of Prudence Trueheart hanging out in a sports bar, wearing a black wig and "seduce me" shoes, was inconceivable.

Whatever the cause, she didn't want these wonder-ful and alarming sensations to end. A secret thrill shot through her, and she grew more determined to take

her pleasure where she could find it—in the sugges-
tive way he looked at her, in her shameless reaction.

"Well?" he asked. "Aren't you going to tell me? Or
do you want me to guess?"

Nora knew the proper etiquette for introductions at
any occasion—except when trying to preserve one's
anonymity beneath a sexy disguise while drinking
champagne with a handsome co-worker at a bar. A
shiver ran up her arm and a moan slipped from her
throat. *A handsome co-worker who was intent on sucking
her fingertips!* That one would surely befuddle even
Emily Post.

One bit of advice did come to mind. When a lady
finds herself in an uncomfortable situation, said lady
can always make a polite retreat to the ladies' room to
regroup. She reached for her purse, reluctantly tugging her trembling fingers away and forcing a smile.
"It was a pleasure meeting you, Mr. Beckett. But I
should go. My friend is probably waiting."

"Your friend can wait. Why don't you want to tell
me your name?" he asked, his smile seductive, his
thumb tracing the line of her jaw. "Are you married?"

Nora gasped and brushed his hand away. How
dare he believe she'd engage in an extramarital flirta-
tion. She'd been brought up better than that! "Of
course not," she said, keeping anger from her voice.

His brow arched teasingly. "Engaged?"

She shook her head.

"Involved?"

Here was her opening, a way to extricate herself
from this situation without making fools of them both.
She cleared her throat and straightened. "If I said yes,
would you leave me alone?"

Pete thought for a moment, then shrugged. "I guess I wouldn't have any choice, would I?"

Nora opened her mouth, ready to lie to him. But the words wouldn't come. She didn't want him to walk away. She wanted him to stay right where he was, to touch her and tease her until she'd had her fill of him. "No," she murmured. "I'm not involved with anyone."

He leaned closer, until his lips were just inches from hers. "Neither am I," he said. "So I guess we're both free to..."

Her gaze fixed on his mouth. "Free to..."

His breath was warm on her lips, taunting her with the promise of one stirring, pulse-pounding kiss. "Free to finish our champagne," he said.

He drew away, leaving her breathless and teetering on the edge of anticipation. A silence grew between them, and her brain scrambled for a topic of conversation to cover her embarrassment. But all she really wanted to discuss was the possibility of his lips meeting hers in the very near future. She grabbed up her champagne glass and gulped down the remaining bubbly. "So, what do you do for a living?" she asked, holding out her glass for a refill. The question was cliché and shallow. Besides that, she already knew the answer. But she wasn't adept at clever conversation, and with him staring into her face, she couldn't think straight.

"You have incredible eyes," he murmured, brushing a strand of hair from her forehead, the same way he'd done that morning. "I don't think I've ever seen eyes quite so blue."

Nora swallowed hard, trying to still the slamming of her heart. How quickly the man forgets, she mused, a trace of anger accompanying the thought. "Oh, I'm sure you have," she said coyly.

He slowly shook his head. "I would have remembered." His fingers wandered to her lips, and he ran his thumb along the corner of her mouth. "So, do you like games?"

"Wha-what?" Her voice cracked slightly at the sudden shift in the conversation. Oh, Lord, he *was* toying with her. All this time, he knew exactly who she was and what she was about, and he was stringing her along! Indignation surged inside her, and she wanted to slap the smirk right off his face.

"Games," he repeated. He glanced up at the television behind the bar. "Sports. This is a sports bar. People who come here, come here for the games. Are you a baseball fan or do you prefer football?"

Nora coughed to cover her uneasiness. "Oh, no," she said, forcing a smile. "I'm not a big sports fan."

"Maybe I could teach you," he said, sliding his hands around her waist. "If you're really interested." Gently, he pressed his palm into the small of her back, drawing her closer. "In most games, there's an offense and a defense." His voice was barely a whisper, his gaze skimming her face. "And the offense does everything it can to break down the defense and...score."

Suddenly, their conversation had taken on a different tone, an undeniable sexual challenge pulsing beneath innocent words. With a trembling hand, Nora reached out and ran her fingers through the hair at his nape, startled by her own boldness. He closed his eyes and tipped his head back, and she stared at him, watching the pleasure suffuse his expression. Her touch had the power to stir his senses, a man so experienced and so worldly. "Nice play," he murmured, watching her through hooded eyes. "I see you understand the concept of offense."

Without another word, he pulled her to her feet, settling her between his legs. She saw a flash of passion in his eyes before his mouth covered hers. She should have been embarrassed to be kissed so brazenly in such a public place. But, instead, she felt wild and uninhibited, completely free of Prudence Trueheart and her stuffy attitudes. She was Nora Pierce again, a woman who could be passionate and spontaneous. A woman who saw what she wanted and kissed it!

Pete's tongue delved into her mouth, and the last shred of her resistance dissolved in his arms. This was the best part of the game, she mused, as he ran his hands along her body. Tantalizing kisses, wanton behavior, with no thought of who they were or how they should behave.

Gently, and then insistently, he probed until she returned his kiss with equal desire. His hands cupped her face, melding her lips to his until the fit was exquisitely perfect, until she knew the taste of him as intimately as she knew the feel of his hands on her and the heat in his eyes.

She placed her palms on his thighs and rubbed, massaging the hard muscle and the warm flesh beneath the fabric of his khakis. Where had she found the courage to match his passion, to tease him with her own? The rest of the world seemed to recede, the din of the bar fading to a distant hum. Finally, when she was certain she couldn't go on any longer, he drew back and gave her a lazy grin.

"That wasn't much of a defense," he teased. "But the game could be interesting, anyway. Why don't we get out of here?"

In a daze, she smiled and wound her arms around his neck. She liked the game, the give and take, and the confidence that made her want to keep playing. "I should probably check on my friend," she said softly, her lips feeling swollen by his tender assault. She'd forgotten all about Ellie, though she wasn't surprised. Pete had a way of focusing every ounce of her attention directly on him. She leaned forward and placed another kiss on his bottom lip, boldly drawing her tongue along the crease of his mouth. "I'll be right back, and then we can leave." She swallowed hard. "Together."

He helped her from the bar stool, grabbing her waist as she stumbled slightly, her knees buckling, still unsteady from their kiss. Then he drew her close and nuzzled her neck. "I'll be right here," he murmured, his breath hot against her ear. "Don't keep me waiting."

As she walked in the direction of the ladies' room, Nora reached up and ran her fingers along her lips, still damp from his kisses. She felt her mouth curve in a naughty smile while a soft giggle slipped from her throat.

"Whatever would Prudence say?" she murmured. Right now, Nora didn't care in the least.

"I CAN'T BELIEVE you're still in here!" Nora stood in front of an open stall in the ladies' room, staring at Ellie Kiley. Her friend had her dress hiked up to her hips and was carefully painting her toenails a bright lavender shade. "Have you been waiting all this time for me?"

Ellie grabbed a wad of toilet paper and stuffed a bit between each toe, then hobbled out of the stall. "I've done my nails twice, plucked my brows and polished all the faucets. I was about to do some minor plumbing repairs when you walked in."

Nora followed her, feeling properly contrite. "Why didn't you leave? You could have escaped without him seeing you."

"Why would I need to escape?" Ellie asked. "He saw me sitting across the bar. I wanted to give you two some time alone before I butted in."

Nora frowned. If Pete had seen Ellie, then certainly he would have put two and two together and come up with "Nora." No, Ellie must be mistaken. He never would have taken such liberties had he realized it was Prudence Trueheart hiding beneath the dark wig and sexy dress.

"I stood outside the ladies' room door and watched you for a while. You two looked so cozy," Ellie said, moving to the sinks. "I figured with all that champagne you were guzzling you'd have to visit the ladies' room sooner or later. Who would have known you'd have a bladder the size of Lake Merced?" Ellie bent down and fanned her toes with her hands. "What did he say when he recognized you? Did he laugh at the wig?"

"The wig is necessary," Nora said, running her fingers through the bangs. "Prudence Trueheart does not hang out in bars looking to pick up men, even if it is for the good of her readers. Besides, it worked, didn't it? No one has recognized me."

"Except for Pete," Ellie clarified.

Nora stared into the mirror above the sinks, watching her reflection with objective eyes. She really didn't look a bit like herself. She looked exotic, sultry, alluring, the dark hair falling around her pale face. Even so, there was her nose—that hadn't changed. And her blue eyes, with the faint trace of a purple bruise beneath the left one. And though her mouth was painted a deep red, it was still her mouth. Nora sent her friend a sideways glance. "Actually, he hasn't recognized me, either."

Ellie's eyes went wide and she gasped. "What? You didn't tell him who you were?"

"I didn't see the point," Nora said. She tugged on the collar of her dress, revealing a bit more shoulder. "Maybe the bustline threw him off." She reached down and readjusted her Miracle Bra, grimacing. "Do you think if I wear this bra for a week, my chest will stay this way?"

When she looked up, she found Ellie staring at her. "What are you saying?" her friend asked, stunned by what she'd seen. "Of course he recognizes you! He'd have to be a dope not to figure it out. You don't look *that* different."

"Well, he doesn't," Nora said. "How could he? He never bothers to look at me at work. He even told me he'd never seen eyes like mine before. I guess he forgot he stared into these same eyes earlier this morning." Drawing a small bottle of perfume from her purse, she dabbed a bit on her neck and between her breasts. "All right, maybe he is just playing along. I don't care. I'm having fun and I like the way he makes me feel."

She enjoyed being the object of his desire, playing the prey to his predator. It made her feel scared and thrilled all at once, as if she possessed some secret power that drew him nearer.

With a snort of disgust, Ellie stepped behind her and yanked the neckline up until the fabric cut into

Nora's armpits. "This isn't just some stranger in a bar. It's Pete Beckett. You work with him. And until recently, you hated him." Ellie grabbed Nora's purse and tucked it under her arm. "Come on. You and I are leaving before you do anything stupid."

Nora snatched her purse from her friend and stubbornly refused to move. "For once in my life, I'd like to do something stupid! I've lived a proper life for twenty-eight years, and look where it's gotten me. I can tell you how to arrange a receiving line at a wedding, how to set a formal table, how to word an engraved invitation. But I can't tell you how it feels to be swept away by passion, to toss aside all common sense and let desire take over. I'm as exciting as a bowl of cold oatmeal."

"Nora, stop and think. This is Pete Beckett. Are you sure you want to become another notch on his bedpost? If you do something stupid tonight, how are you going to face him tomorrow morning?"

"I don't care," Nora said. "That's the wonderful thing about doing something truly stupid. You're *supposed* to regret it the next morning. You regret it, then forget it. Besides, he doesn't know who I am. If he did, he would have said something by now. Especially after he kissed me."

Ellie's eyes went wide. "Pete Beckett kissed you?"

"More than once," Nora said smugly. "And he sucked on my fingers." She sighed deeply. "I thought I'd faint."

Her friend frowned and shook her head, staring at her in the mirror. "Maybe he doesn't recognize you. Pete Beckett never would have sucked on Prudence Trueheart's fingers." A bemused expression settled on Ellie's face. "Sam's never sucked on my fingers."

"Well, it feels good. And what's wrong with enjoying the moment? Who could it hurt?"

Ellie wrapped her arm around Nora's shoulders. "I know how nice it is to feel wanted. And it's been a long time since you've been with a man. But a one-night stand with Pete Beckett is not going to help matters."

"It's been three years," Nora said. "If you don't count Stuart."

Stuart Anderson was Nora's landlord and closest male friend. For the past three years, Stuart had been her escort to all her mother's high-society parties and fund-raisers. Celeste Pierce fancied Stuart as a son-in-law. With his impeccable manners and smooth social skills, he'd fit right in with Celeste's crowd.

"I like Stuart," Ellie said. "He's safe and dependable. Not like Pete Beckett. Why don't you sleep with him?"

"Stuart is gay," Nora replied. "I don't think he'll be sucking my fingers anytime soon." A deep sigh slipped from her lips. It wasn't just the sex that she longed for with a man. She wanted all the simple sensations that went with it. The wonderful feel of a man's weight on her body, the smooth skin and the hard muscle beneath her palms. The narrow hips that fit so perfectly between her legs and the heady awareness of his body moving inside hers. She wanted to experience all that just once more before she died—or turned thirty! And she was about to throw away her one and only chance.

"If I wanted to have a one-night stand, this would be the perfect opportunity," Nora said. "I can just disappear from his life as if I never existed. He won't even have to take the trouble to give me his usual brush-off. And better yet, I know him and so do you. He's not some deranged psycho or an escaped ax murderer. I don't have to worry about my safety."

Ellie shook her head. "Nora, please, don't—"

"I can control my emotions," she said. "I'm a big girl, Ellie. I know what I'm doing."

"But what about your heart?" Ellie asked. "Can you promise that you won't have feelings for him later on?"

"Of course I won't. He's Pete Beckett. And I'm—well, you know who I am. I'm Prudence Trueheart and I couldn't possibly fall in love with a man like him." Nora drew a ragged breath, then forced a smile. "Maybe you're worried if he realizes I'm Prudence Trueheart, he'll be so repulsed he won't want to kiss me or touch me."

"No! Honey, I'm just saying this is a dangerous game you're playing and if you let it go on, the only one who stands to get hurt is you. Remember, he's the expert here and you're just a...rookie."

Nora cursed inwardly, impatient with Ellie's pleas. "All right," she said, flipping on the faucet to wash her hands. "I'm not going to let it go any further. I'll go back out there and tell him I'm going home with you. And that will be the end of it."

Ellie nodded and squeezed Nora's shoulder. "Now you're talking sensibly. After all, he's bound to guess who you are when you...well, if you get intimate. Or when he sobers up, whichever comes first."

Nora tossed the paper towel in the wastebasket, then walked to the door. But she stopped before walking out. Maybe Ellie was right. Objectively, she never would have recommended what she was contemplating—a single night of passion, a one-night stand. But she was sick to death of thinking like Prudence. For once, she wanted to break all the rules—and damn the consequences.

"All right," she repeated softly. "I'm just going to say goodbye and then we can leave." As she opened the bathroom door, she glanced over her shoulder at her friend, who was bending to remove the toilet paper from between her toes. "You're a very good nag. If I ever leave the *Herald*, I'm going to recommend you for the job as Prudence. You're beginning to sound more like her than I do!"

3

PETE KNEW she wouldn't be back. She'd find a rear door and slip out without saying another word to him, leaving him to wonder what he'd done wrong. Tomorrow, at the office, she'd act as if nothing had happened. And perhaps another night, she'd put on the dress and the wig and the sexy heels and try again, this time with a real stranger.

A surge of jealousy pulsed through him as he thought about the next man she'd meet and seduce. He fought the urge to go after her, to call an end to the charade. The game had gone far enough. There was a certain allure in seducing a complete stranger, but both of them knew they were far from strangers.

Was that what she'd been looking for tonight? Anonymous sex? Did she hide behind the Prudence Trueheart facade by day, only to turn into a wanton woman by night? Pete's jaw tightened and he cursed. The hell if he was going to let her do this again! He'd walk right into her office tomorrow morning and threaten her with exposure. Sure, it was a rash step, but she couldn't be putting herself in danger like this again—he damn well wouldn't allow it.

What if he'd been some creep with notches in his bedposts? Some guy intent on dragging her home and ravishing her, then dumping her without a second thought? Pete winced inwardly. The description might have applied to him at one time. But Nora Pierce wasn't the type of woman a guy loved and left. She was different. Special. There was a vulnerability behind her tremulous smile that made him want to protect her, rather than take advantage.

Maybe it would be better to go directly to Ellie, Pete mused. After all, she'd accompanied Nora to the bar. Certainly, she'd have some influence on Nora's behavior. And if Ellie wasn't cooperative, he'd enlist Sam's help. Pete spun around on his bar stool and ordered a whiskey, neat. When the bartender delivered the drink, Pete gulped it down and ordered another. "This is the end of the game, Prudence," Pete murmured, his throat burning from the whiskey. "And I'm the last man you're going to play with."

He thought about how he'd broach the subject. She'd probably be angry at his interference, maybe even order him out of her office. By the rules, he'd be required to pretend that nothing had happened between them. That was all part of her little game. At any moment, Pete had expected her to reveal herself, but, instead, she'd fallen deeper into the charade. She was at times coy and flirtatious, then sexy and seductive.

She wasn't Prudence Trueheart. Hell, she wasn't even Nora Pierce anymore. She was a stranger whom Pete found endlessly attractive and intriguing. And she played the role with great enthusiasm. He noticed her wrap, still draped across the back of her bar stool and he idly fingered the soft cashmere, recalling the feel of her skin, the taste of her mouth.

He'd never expected her touch to affect him so profoundly. Nothing had prepared him for his reaction when her fingers skimmed his thighs, her palms just inches away from his unbidden erection. For that brief moment, they'd existed in a fantasy world, in a place where real life didn't dare intrude, where her touch and the sound of her voice slowly stoked his desire until he could barely contain the fire.

By the time she'd walked away, he'd almost been relieved to have been saved from certain embarrassment. They'd reached their limit and the only place left to venture was into more intimate territory. And though he didn't want the evening to end, he knew it had to.

Pete swirled his second whiskey in the tumbler, looking to the amber liquid for answers. But the drink couldn't quell the desire that still racked his body. Liquor just softened the edge a little. It would take a lot more than whiskey to forget this night, he mused. This was the stuff that male fantasies were made of—at least, until she walked out on him.

But what the hell was he supposed to do now? He couldn't pretend it hadn't happened. And he wasn't about to go in to the office tomorrow and ignore her the way he had for the past three years. Maybe there'd be some silent acknowledgment between them, a wordless understanding that this night had never—

"Ready?"

Pete froze at the sound of her voice, the drink halfway to his lips. Slowly, he turned around to find Nora standing behind him, shifting nervously from foot to foot. She clutched her purse in white-knuckled hands, and a tight smile curled her lushly painted lips.

"Ready for what?" he asked.

A blush worked its way up her cheeks, and she glanced over her shoulder. "I thought you wanted to leave. We should go. Right now."

Her tone was insistent, and he wasn't about to ar-
gue with her, no matter how stunned he was. Pete
dropped his glass on the bar, spattering whisky on his
jacket sleeve, and jumped up. "Right," he said, trying
to cover his surprise. "I'm ready. Let's go." He
grabbed her wrap and gently steered her toward the
door, trying to figure out how he'd completely mis-
read her intentions. She couldn't really plan to take
this evening to its most logical conclusion, could she?
This was Prudence Trueheart he was with! But, then,
he'd recently begun to learn that Nora Pierce was *not*
Prudence Trueheart.

The air was cool and damp when they got outside, a
mist rolling in from the nearby Bay and softening the
focus of their surroundings. Pedestrians strolled
through the courtyard of the Cannery, among fragrant
olive trees and the sounds of street musicians. As they
walked out to Jefferson Street, the fresh smell of salt-
water mixed with the mouth-watering scents of seafood. The last of the Dungeness crab was being sold
out of the outdoor crab pots.

In the distance, the rumble from the Hyde Street cable car came out of the dark. They stood on the sidewalk for a moment, then Nora glanced nervously over
at him. "Do—do you have a car?" she asked.

"Do you?" he countered.

Nora shook her head. "I came with my friend."

Pete chuckled. His place was a brisk twenty-minute
walk from the Wharf and parking was impossible
within the city limits, so he'd left his car at home.
"Well, this is embarrassing," Pete muttered. "I
walked here. I live just south, on Russian Hill. We
could go to your place if it's closer."

She shook her head. "We'll go to your place," she said emphatically. "I can call a cab from there."

So this was the plan, he mused. She'd get him alone and then drop the bomb on his home turf. Damn, he wanted to call an end to this right now! He wanted to demand an explanation. But, instead, he decided to bide his time. Pete draped her wrap around her shoulders, then took her hand in his and pointed down the street. "It's too far to walk. We'll take the cable car."

The Hyde Street line took them within a few blocks of his condo on Macondray Lane, so they hopped the next car that passed and found a spot to stand in the rear. She held on to the bar overhead, and he stood behind her, his feet braced against the sway of the car and his arms wrapped around her waist. Her backside nestled against his lap, brushing against him until he thought he'd groan from the torment. He fought the dull ache growing in his groin, fought the swell of heat and the frantic need to touch her and find his release. By the time they reached the top of Russian Hill, he could barely keep his hands off her.

The car stopped on the corner of Hyde and Green, and Pete helped her off, grabbing her waist and swinging her down from the step. Her body slid along the length of his, and for a moment, he lost himself in the tantalizing feel of her hips pressed into his. Then he gently pushed her into the shadows of a high wall and grabbed her face in his hands. He kissed her long and deep, desperate with need, his hips flush against hers. This night was not going to end well. There were bound to be angry words and nasty accusations, but right now, he wanted to savor every moment he had with her.

Pete felt her shudder and he stepped back and looked down into her eyes. "Are you all right?"

Nora nodded, her teeth working at her lower lip. "I'm just a little cold."

Pete shrugged his shoulders and slipped out of his sports jacket, then wrapped it around her. She gave him a sweet smile, and he tugged gently at the lapels, dropping a kiss on her lips. God, why couldn't they have been strangers? he wondered. Everything would have been a lot less complicated. They could have gone to his place, made passionate love, and then exchanged phone numbers at the end of the night.

With his hand splayed on her back, he steered her in the direction of his condo, all the while wishing they could just stay on the street and continue the charade a little longer. He wanted more time with Nora Pierce, time to figure out what was happening between them. By all accounts, he shouldn't want her at all. She was exactly the type of woman he took great pains to avoid. But with every moment he spent near her, he found himself looking at her in a different light.

They passed the short walk to his place in silence. She hesitated once on the steps in front of the condo, and he waited for her, wondering if she'd reveal herself now—praying that she wouldn't. He pushed the key into the lock, then turned the knob and stepped aside to let Nora pass. She stopped just inside the door, and for a moment, he thought she'd turn and run.

"It's...very nice," she murmured, her gaze darting around the dim interior as she slipped out of his sport coat.

Pete closed the door softly behind him, then leaned against it, afraid that any sudden movement might spook her. "This is what four years in the majors bought me. This and a bum knee."

She didn't comment, didn't even turn around. Hell, she knew all about his baseball career, everyone at the paper did. Yet, if they were strangers, she should at least be a little curious. It was the first crack in her charade, and he wondered if she was finally ready to admit who she was. He decided to press the issue.

"I still don't know your name."

She stiffened, and he reached out to place his palms on her shoulders, gently massaging her nape with his fingers, his hands twisted in the soft fabric of her wrap. Then she released a long breath and sank back against him. Unable to stop himself, Pete nuzzled her neck, drawing her hair back before pressing a kiss right below her ear.

He felt the wild thrum of her pulse, heard her quickened breathing. His lips drifted along her bare shoulder, and he gave her a gentle nip, then slowly stepped back, waiting for the big revelation, the moment when she either ran like a rabbit or revealed her identity. But the moment didn't come.

She turned around slowly. "No names," she said, her voice low and even. "For now, let's just forget about manners and etiquette. Let's just be strangers."

"Surely you have a name," he insisted, running his thumb along her lower lip.

He knew he was pushing, but he never expected her to push back. With a soft oath, she threw her arms around his neck, rose up on her toes and pressed her mouth to his. At first, the kiss was clumsy and fierce, meant to silence his inquisition, but his own response was instant and intense. Her tongue grazed his teeth, and he let her have control for just a moment, allowing the sweet heat to twist in the pit of his stomach and radiate through his body.

Where had all this desire come from? Just this morning they'd faced off over an errant baseball and a black eye. And now, all he could think about was the feel of her skin beneath his palms, the way her naked body might look beneath that sexy dress. Heat blazed through his bloodstream, and another surge of need clouded his common sense.

With a low moan, Pete grabbed her around the waist and pressed her back against the front door, covering her mouth with his. She writhed against him, her hands skimming frantically over his shoulders and chest. Her touch threatened to obliterate every ounce of his restraint, and he snatched her wrists up and pinned them above her head.

She had to stop; he had to give her every opportunity to rethink her actions. He wasn't going to be sorry for this in the morning, and neither would she. He'd make sure of that. Pete drew back and looked into her eyes, his gaze scanning her flushed face, her damp lips. Those lips, so warm, so sweet. He craved the taste, like a man dying of hunger.

A moan rumbled in his chest and he released her wrists and crushed his body into hers, kissing her long and deep. But she didn't turn away. Instead, Nora matched his kiss with unfettered passion of her own, arching against him. He wasn't prepared for it to feel so good, his hips rocking against hers, his shaft hard and aching for release.

Slowly, deliciously, he seduced her with his tongue, moving from her mouth to her neck and onto the warm valley between her breasts. With insistent fingers, he tugged at the neckline of her dress until the lacy edge of her bra was revealed, and then the pink tip of her breast. Surely, she'd stop him now, before he took such intimate liberties. But she said nothing, her quickened breath and her soft moans urging him forward.

She had a perfect body, Pete mused, made for his hands. He wanted to pause for a moment and take it all in. To memorize the way his palm cupped her breast, the way her nipple hardened beneath his thumb. Everything about her made him yearn to possess her completely, yet they were still nothing more than strangers.

Nora's breath caught as he drew her nipple into his mouth, and he paused. But rather than pull away, she melted into him, pressing her palms against the door and offering no resistance. His lips teased at the hardened nub, nuzzled the warm flesh, every thought focused on giving her pleasure. With other women, he'd always gone through the motions of foreplay, but with Nora, he wanted her to truly need him, to ache for him the same way he ached for her, until he became the only man who could satisfy her completely.

But she soon grew impatient with his lazy seduction. With a soft cry, she reached out and tugged at his tie, unknotting it, then tossing it aside. The simple act of undressing him elevated his desire. But when she reached for the buttons of his shirt, Pete grabbed her wrists and pulled them away. This had gone too damn far, and he was too close to losing control! She was going to stop, of that he was sure. He just didn't want her to stop when he was standing naked in front of her.

"Tell me what you want," he said, his jaw tight. "Say it."

Her eyes were glassy and heavy-lidded, her lips

moist, puffy. She hardly looked like a woman determined to embarrass him. "You," she finally murmured, the tiny plea coming from deep in her throat as she curled against him. He let her hands go, and she slowly undid the buttons, then nuzzled her face into his chest.

This should feel all wrong, he thought to himself, tipping his head back and enjoying the warmth of her tongue. But everything about it felt right, as if this was somehow meant to happen between them. Her teeth grazed his nipple, and he sucked in a sharp breath. "How much further are you going to let this go?" he asked, his voice low. "Because if it goes any further than this, I can't guarantee I'll be able to stop."

She skimmed her fingers over his chest, her head bent. "I know what I'm doing," she said, her tone firm, confident. "And I don't want to stop."

Pete caught her chin and tipped her head up until he met her gaze. Suddenly, he wanted it all to be real. The fantasy wasn't enough—passion between strangers meant nothing to him. He wanted to look into her eyes and know that he saw Nora there. And he wanted her to say his name, soft and urgent, with every wave of passion that surged between them. But he could only take what she offered. He'd have to deal with all the questions he had later.

With a groan, he grabbed the front of his shirt and yanked it off, pulling his hands from the still-buttoned cuffs. Then he braced his palms on either side of her head and kissed her again, his mouth hard and demanding, unyielding. If she wanted him, she'd have to take him on his own terms. And the only requirement he had was that he'd damn well make sure this wasn't the last time they ever made love.

He wanted to take her into the bedroom, to seduce her slowly and completely. But as he kissed her and touched her, all reason seemed to disappear. They'd jumped onto a runaway train, and stopping now was impossible, even though they were heading for trouble. Each caress became more frantic, more needy, and Pete knew they couldn't wait much longer. He bunched his fists in the hem of her dress and drew it up along her thighs, then ran his fingers under the edge of her lacy panties.

Emboldened, she raked her nails along his chest, drifting lower until she reached his belly. Her hands no longer trembled as she worked his belt open and when she unzipped his pants, her fingers brushed against the hard ridge beneath the smooth fabric of his khakis. They touched each other at the same time, her fingers closing over his rigid shaft as his pushed aside her panties and dipped to the moist heat between her legs. That they were still partially dressed only added to the fierce need for immediate release and the forbidden nature of what they were about to do.

"Tell me your name," he demanded, slowly rubbing his fingertip over her sex. "I need to say your name when I move inside you."

But she couldn't answer. Already her breathing had gone shallow and her body tense. He knew he could bring her to release with just his fingers, but Pete wanted more. He drew his hand away, then grabbed a condom from his wallet. He rolled it on himself, knowing that if she touched him again he'd be lost. Then he grabbed her thighs and pulled them up along his hips, pressing her body back into the door. "Tell me this is what you want," he murmured, desperation edging his voice. "Tell me!"

Nora wrapped her legs around his waist, arching her back until his erection grazed the damp heat of her opening. "Yes," she said, sinking down until he'd barely penetrated her. "I want this. I want you." She took a shaky breath. "Now."

Pete couldn't believe they'd gone so far, but he couldn't hold back any longer. If he didn't take her now, he'd be lost. With ruthless control, he slowly drove inside her, delicious sensation coursing through his body as she sheathed him, her sex tight and hot. Almost immediately, he felt her swell around him and tremble with the first signs of her climax.

Closing his eyes, he moved, driving deeper with each thrust and then slowly withdrawing. He'd never had this with a woman before, this undeniable need to possess not only her body, but her soul. It made him angry and alive at the same time. Nora was his now, and he wasn't going to give her up, not until he was ready.

Drawing a deep breath, he stilled his movement, then gazed into her face. At that moment, as she teetered on the edge of ecstasy, her eyes closed, her lips parted, he knew he'd never known a more beautiful, desirable woman. He wanted the moment to last, that instant they became one and he saw inside her soul. But then he felt her convulse around him and his control shattered in a single instant.

He said her name just once, at the moment of his own climax. But she was in the midst of her own splintering orgasm, and he knew she hadn't heard him. Time seemed to slow, that moment spinning out around them, wrapping them in a cocoon of wellsated hunger. Pete stroked her hair and kissed her neck as they slowly drifted back into reality. At that instant, he would have given five years of his life to stop time, to languish in the aftermath without the threat of real life intruding.

"Words fail me," he murmured with a soft chuckle. "I usually know exactly what to say."

She didn't move, didn't speak, as he disposed of the condom. When he looked at her again, the passion had already begun to fade from her expression. With every breath she took, realization tugged at them both, driving them apart. He kissed her again, hoping to stop it, but nothing he did could alter the truth of what they'd just done.

It was there in her eyes—the fear, the regret, the guilt. Instead of wanting to bask in the afterglow, she wanted to escape. Pete's heart twisted in his chest and he scrambled for the right words to say, the best way to reach her and convince her to stay. But he already knew the consequences of what they'd shared, and he had to force himself to let go. Slowly, Pete backed away, and she slid along his body until her feet were on the floor.

"I—I've got to go," Nora murmured, pushing her skirt down.

"Don't," he countered, reaching out to cup her face in his hands. "I want you to stay."

"No," she replied, evading his touch. "I really have to go."

He should have been angry, but all he could muster was resignation. "I'll drive you," he said, knowing full well she'd refuse. God, he couldn't even offer her a ride home, standard courtesy for a woman he'd just made love to. He rezipped his pants, then looked around for his discarded shirt.

"I have an early day tomorrow," she said, by way of an excuse, "and—and I have to pack."

Pete regarded her with a suspicious eye. This was a new tactic. Up until this point, she hadn't really lied, only skirted the truth. He knew damn well Prudence Trueheart didn't travel. She hadn't had a vacation in years. "Are you going somewhere?"

"Um...Pakistan," she blurted out, obviously naming the first far-off place that came to mind. "Very important business trip. A long, long business trip. I won't be back for... Well, I'm not sure when I'll be back."

"Pakistan," Pete muttered, barely able to contain a laugh. "Do you expect me to—"

"Of course, I don't expect you to wait for me!" Nora said, snatching her purse and wrap up from the floor. "I'll call you when I get back, though." She brushed an awkward kiss on his cheek, paused for a moment, then turned to the door.

Pete pulled it open for her. "You don't know my phone number."

She glanced over her shoulder and blinked, then forced a lighthearted giggle. "Then I guess you'll have to call me!" With that, she hurried out the door and down the front steps of his condo. She didn't bother to look back, didn't seem to realize that he had followed her out.

He watched her until she disappeared into the thin mist. He had no choice but to let her go, Pete mused, the night air cold on his bare chest. But he knew this wasn't over between them. A man didn't make love to a woman like Nora Pierce and just forget her. There would be other nights between them. But he'd make sure that things would be different. They'd never be strangers again.

NORA'S HEELS CLICKED on the deserted sidewalk, echoing in the chilly night mist. She glanced back only once, and though Pete's condo had already faded from view, her skin was still damp from the heat of their frantic joining, her lips still warm from his kisses. Her heart slammed in her chest and her head spun. She wanted to stop and draw a deep, calming breath. But she was afraid to give herself even a moment to regret her actions.

She'd expected to feel some measure of triumph. Her three-year bout of celibacy was over, and she'd ended it in grand style, with a man who had made the experience more than memorable. But try as she might, Nora couldn't sort out her jumbled emotions. Exhilaration was mixed with regret, relief was tinged with apprehension. A shiver ran down her spine, and she drew her wrap more tightly around her as she walked.

It had been quite wonderful. In truth, beyond anything she could have imagined. They had been wild and frantic, their hunger so primal that nothing could stand in the way of sating their lust, not even a few layers of clothing. A tiny smile quirked her lips, and she pressed her palm to her chest. The adrenaline still coursed through her body, and she knew if she had stayed with him, they would have made love all over again.

Nora stopped, then turned around. She fought the urge to go back, but this time common sense prevailed. Once would have to be enough, though twice certainly sounded tempting. With a soft moan, she continued down the sidewalk to Union Street. Her shoes, so sexy in front of her bedroom mirror, now pinched and rubbed, a painful reminder that at the end of the night she would shed the trappings of her one-night stand as easily as she had shed her inhibitions.

Though the dress and dark wig had done the job, she now felt conspicuous, as if everyone she passed on the street knew exactly what she'd been up to. The hem rode up on her thighs, and the chilly air cut through the cashmere wrap until her whole body began to tremble. She made it as far as Washington Square before her wobbly knees gave out and she had to sit down on a park bench.

Bracing her elbows on her knees, she cupped her chin in her hands and drew a long breath. The park, in the heart of Little Italy, was ringed with Italian restaurants, and the night air was filled with the scent of garlic and sweet tomato sauce. Nora closed her eyes and fought the tremors that raced through her body.

Oh, Lord, what had she done? She'd been wild and shameless, with no regard for modesty. But then, he had no idea that he'd made love to Prudence Trueheart. She should be able to walk right past him tomorrow without a qualm, putting the entire experience in the past—if not for the fact that she remembered every perfect detail of their time together, from the heat of his breath on her neck to the sensation of his moving inside her.

How could she have been so stupid? She'd assumed the experience of making love to Pete Beckett would be easy to put behind her. If the intensity of those memories even diminished by half by the next morning, Nora would still be in trouble. "I'll have to call in

sick," she murmured. "Maybe even contract a pro-
longed illness—malaria or consumption."

Reaching in her purse for change, Nora hobbled
over to the bus stop. She wasn't far from home, but her
feet just didn't want to go another four or five blocks.
She still had to climb halfway down the steep Filbert
steps to reach her apartment on Darrell Place.

Muni was nearly empty when she boarded, and she
took a spot near the front, behind an elderly lady.
Wincing against the harsh glare of the lights, Nora
tugged on her skirt and pulled at the neckline of her
dress—a dress suddenly much more revealing than
she remembered it. Her mind flashed an image of Pete
running his hands along her thighs, bunching her skirt
in his fists, and Nora felt her face flood with heat. She
glanced around to see if anyone had noticed, then
pulled her wrap up to her ears and sank down in her
seat.

With every ounce of willpower she possessed, she
tried to put it all out of her mind. But every image,
every feeling had imprinted itself on her brain until it
had become a part of her. Seeing him again, watching
him from a distance, could only make those feelings
more acute.

She should have listened to Ellie and walked out of
that bar when she had the chance. What had happened to her common sense? And Prudence—where
had she disappeared to? Nora couldn't count the
number of letters she'd received from victims of The
One-Night Stand. And her advice had always been the
same: don't be stupid, ignore your hormones and use
your head. Yet a bottle of champagne and a boyish
grin was all it had taken for her to forget everything
Prudence had taught her.

When the bus circled Coit Tower, she got off, removing her shoes the moment her feet hit the cool sidewalk. Frustrated, she picked up the offending footwear and threw the heels into a nearby hydrangea bush. "Good riddance," she muttered, setting off down the hill. When she reached Darrell Place, she ripped off the wig and tucked it beneath her arm.

What was wrong with her? She'd made a decision to give in to passion, and though she had a few regrets, surely she could put her night with Pete in perspective. "It was purely physical," she murmured as she approached her house. She opened her purse and fished for her keys. Just as she found them, a voice sounded from behind her.

"Look at you. You are so bad!"

With a tiny scream, Nora spun around, the keys slipping from her fingers and dropping into a rhododendron at the base of the front steps. Her palm flew to her chest and her heart leapt into her throat. "Stuart! Good grief, you scared me."

Her landlord scowled as he came into the light spilling from the front porch. A slight figure, he wore a colorful silk robe and held pruning shears in his hand.

From the moment Nora had moved into the tiny attic apartment on the third floor of Stuart's house, he'd barged into her life and made himself welcome, becoming one of her trusted confidants. At any given time, he'd served as her surrogate brother, sister, mother or father—as well as her party escort. "What are you doing up so late? More midnight gardening?"

"The question is," Stuart said, "what have *you* been doing? I'd wager it wasn't gardening, although someone was sowing his seed."

"I don't know what you mean," Nora said, brushing by him.

"You've had sex," Stuart said in a matter-of-fact voice.

Nora clapped her palms to her cheeks and spun around. "You can tell? Just by looking at me? Oh, God, I didn't think it would be *that* obvious!"

Stuart waved his hand. "Honey, you've got a glow about you as bright as Coit Tower." He chuckled. "They could put you out on Alcatraz and use you as a lighthouse. Or maybe the city could—"

"Enough." Nora moaned and dropped into the soft cushions of the porch swing. Suddenly, she didn't have the energy to climb two flights to her attic apartment. Stuart sat down beside her and gave her knee a sympathetic pat. "Tell Uncle Stuart all about it. And don't leave out any of the details."

Nora gave him a halfhearted smile, then drew a deep breath. "Well...it was wonderful. Passionate. Mind-boggling. And I think it might have been the biggest mistake of my life."

"Honey, passion is never a mistake. Don't you know that?"

"That's what I thought. But I'm afraid this was." Nora turned to Stuart. "I made love...to Pete Beckett."

Stuart's eyes went wide. "That dishy sports columnist? The one with the cute butt and the broad shoulders? I've always had a crush on him."

"That's the one," Nora said. "Only, he didn't know it was me." She held out the wig. "This was incognito passion."

Stuart took the wig, ran his fingers through it, then placed it on his slightly balding head. He sighed dramatically, crossed his legs at the knee and neatly arranged his hands over the hem of his robe. "Girlfriend, welcome to the world of unrequited lust. I'll be your tour guide. If you have any questions, don't be shy. Just ask."

Nora couldn't help but giggle. "Maybe it's not so bad."

Stuart reached around her and gave her shoulder a squeeze. "Of course it's not. Now, about those details."

"I mean, I can walk into the office tomorrow and pretend as if nothing happened."

"Details," Stuart repeated.

"It's not like we might have had a future together. We couldn't possibly date. He's not my type!"

"Oh, but honey, he's *my* type. Now, about those details."

Nora turned to Stuart. "I can do this," she said, her attitude brightening. "It might be difficult at first, but I can forget Pete Beckett and everything that happened between us." She pushed off the swing, adjusted her cashmere wrap and sighed deeply. "Thank you, Stuart. Talking to you always helps." Nora started for the stairs, then turned and blew Stuart a kiss.

"You're a fickle wench," Stuart said, pouting. "One night of passion and you forget all about your friend Stuart."

Nora laughed. "Don't be silly. You're still the only man in my life."

"Don't lie to me, you hussy. I was perusing *Town and Country* and noticed that Celeste is throwing her opera orgy in a couple of weeks. You didn't even bother to mention the party to me."

Nora smiled. "I got my invitation last week. An alfresco dinner on the terrace for eighty of her closest and richest friends. You'll be my escort?''

Stuart clapped excitedly. ''Of course! I've had my eye on a new tuxedo. An Armani. And of course, you'll tell Celeste that I'm coming. Last time, she consulted me on the seating arrangements. I was quite helpful. And I have to tell her about a new florist I stumbled upon. Exquisite arrangements. Oh, and I saw the most wonderful gown at a little boutique off Union Square. The color would be perfect for Celeste.''

''Stuart, you're the daughter she never had. And if you were a plastic surgeon, you'd be the son-in-law she's always wanted.'' Nora shook her head. She wandered back to the porch swing and brushed a grateful kiss on Stuart's cheek. ''You're the kind of man I'm looking for. Refined, dependable, understanding. Too bad you're not straight. I'd marry you in a minute.''

As she turned to climb the stairs, she heard Stuart chuckle. ''Honey, you don't know what you want. But I think you're about to find out.''

Nora stopped on the stairs and turned to look at Stuart. But all she saw was his front door closing behind him. She frowned, wondering at his meaning. She might not know what she wanted, but she knew what she *didn't* want. She didn't want her mind plagued with thoughts of Pete Beckett. She didn't want her breath to catch or her heart to pound whenever she saw him.

''I just don't want to want him!'' she cried, taking the last flight of steps two at a time.

4

PETE WAS JUST ABOUT TO GIVE UP on Nora when he suddenly spied her skulking through the office in dark glasses and a beige trench coat. If she thought she was inconspicuous, she was sorely mistaken. To blend into the Bullpen, faded jeans, an old football jersey, and a Giants baseball cap were standard uniform. But even if she had been dressed casually, she still wouldn't have gotten past him. He'd been waiting all morning for her to arrive, waiting all morning with thoughts of her spinning in his mind and flooding his senses.

He watched as she hurried into her office and closed the door behind her, her mouth—the same mouth that had driven him wild last night, the same lips that had tasted like sweet wine—set in a grim line. Thoughts of all they'd shared had taunted his dreams, and he'd spent a fitful night trying to reconcile his impulsive actions and her surprising reactions.

Now, he was ready to straighten everything out. They'd start with her rather dangerous habit of picking up strange men in bars. Certainly Nora couldn't be so naive that she didn't understand the risks. The woman wrote an advice column! But perhaps she really wasn't as street-smart as he'd assumed. Nora's advice tended to be more about open-toed shoes after Memorial Day and the dress code for a felony trial, than issues of promiscuity. He'd noticed the subject of sex had cropped up more often lately, though, but suspected that trend wasn't her doing.

He'd have to word his warning carefully, deftly avoiding his own complicity in the matter and ignoring that he'd done exactly what he was warning her against—picked up a stranger. But then, she wasn't really a stranger, was she? Once he admitted he knew her identity from the start, his motives were in the clear, weren't they?

Pete paused, his hand on the door to her office, a frown creasing his brow. But if he knew it was Nora beneath the wig and sexy black dress, then how would he explain seducing her in the bar? Did he really seduce her just to protect her? That question banged around in his brain for a few seconds before he realized he was damned whichever way he turned.

The only way to escape without incurring her wrath was to act as if he'd really and truly made love to a stranger last night. He'd have to continue the charade *and* figure out a way to keep her from prowling the singles bars at night.

A soft oath slipped from his lips. Why the hell did he care what she did with her free time? It wasn't as if Nora was his responsibility. By all rights, they barely knew each other. But from the moment he'd beaned her with a baseball, he'd felt an undeniable connection between them. And after last night, he wasn't willing to share her with any other man.

Pete raised his hand to knock, but then decided surprise was the best tactic. He silently pushed the door open in front of him and he found her, still wrapped in her coat and wearing her glasses, stuffing papers into her briefcase and muttering to herself.

"I was wondering when you'd get in." He smiled as

Nora jumped, a tiny scream slipping from her throat. The papers she held slipped to the floor, and she bent down to retrieve them, bashing her head on the edge of her desk in the process and knocking her sunglasses askew.

Pete circled her desk and bent down to help her. "Late night?"

She glanced up over the rims of her glasses. "Wha-what?"

"It's nearly lunchtime. You're wearing sunglasses inside. If I didn't know you better, I'd say you were out last night and had a little too much to drink." He slipped her sunglasses off and gazed into her wide eyes. Myriad emotions radiated from their blue depths—fear, apprehension, and a tiny flicker of desire. "Weren't quite ready to face the day this morning?"

Nervously, she clambered to her feet and shoved the papers in a file folder. "Actually, I'm doing quite well."

Pete rose, then sat down on the edge of her desk. "Then you must have had a good time last night."

She sucked in a sharp breath, her face going pale. For a moment, she forgot to exhale. He was about to slap her back, when she finally spoke.

"Last night?"

She wasn't going to reveal herself, Pete mused. Nora was going to pretend that nothing had happened between them! "Yes, your date. Remember, the black eye. You said you had a date."

"I did not," Nora murmured. She grimaced, then sent him an irritated glare. "What's with all the questions? What do you want? Why are you here?"

With single-minded purpose, he reached out and

touched the bruise on her cheekbone. "I wanted to check up on you." Such an innocent thing, to brush his fingers over her skin. But his reaction was immediate and intense, and Pete fought the urge to cup her pretty face in his hands and kiss her, to lose himself in the sweet taste of her mouth. Maybe then, she'd finally admit her deception. "Hmm, doesn't sound like you had a very good time," he said.

"I don't know what you're talking about," she replied.

Nora gave a nonchalant shrug, but he could tell she was having trouble maintaining her composure—and the illusion that she'd put last night behind her. Her perfect nose flared slightly and her lower lip trembled. What would be so bad about admitting their attraction to each other? Did she regret their time together so much that she had to push it from her mind?

Pete chuckled, then shoved off her desk. Or was this all part of the game? Was he supposed to want her more just because she didn't acknowledge that he'd wanted her last night? He stretched out in one of her guest chairs and watched her intently. Or was Nora still under the delusion that he hadn't recognized her beneath the dark wig?

"Well, at least one of us had a good time last night."

Her head snapped up and she blinked, clutching her file folder with white-knuckled hands. "You went out?" she asked.

Pete nodded. "I met the most incredible woman."

"I wa—I mean, she was?" Color tinged her cheeks, and she gnawed at her lower lip. She carefully composed herself, playing at indifference, schooling her voice into a blasé tone. "What made her so...incredible?"

"She's sexy as hell," he said. He leaned back in his chair and laced his fingers behind his head. He watched as her eyes drifted to his shirt, pulled tight across his chest, lingering there for a moment. When her gaze drifted lower, Pete cleared his throat, and she looked up, embarrassed. "Beautiful," he continued. "Smart, funny, interesting. I've never met anyone like her."

"Maybe you've been dating the wrong kind of woman," Nora said.

"She had these incredible eyes." Pete leaned forward and braced his arms on her desk. "You know, your eyes are almost the same color. But not quite the right shade." He could barely maintain a straight face. Nora looked downright insulted by the backhanded compliment. "And she was about your size, only much...curvier." Why not twist the knife a little? "And her mouth, well, she—"

"I'm sure I don't need all the details," Nora said. "Don't you have some work to do? Or some game to play? Why are you here?"

An idea slowly grew in his mind, a way to keep Nora to himself until she was ready to put an end to her little game. "Actually, I could use some advice. You're good at that sort of thing, aren't you? You are an advice columnist."

"I'm an etiquette columnist. And I'm sure I couldn't possibly give Pete Beckett dating advice."

"But you'd be the perfect person," Pete insisted. "You see, I'm in a rather delicate position. Usually when I meet a woman, there's an instant physical attraction."

"I really don't—"

"And though I try to take things slowly, I often ignore common sense and just...plunge right in." The last was said slowly, provocatively, causing a blush to rise in her cheeks. Pete wondered how much more of this she could take before cracking.

"Please, there's really nothing I can—"

"What's the etiquette for a one-night stand?" he asked, his query blunt and to the point—and purely for effect.

Her color deepened and she gasped, her jaw dropping. "What?"

"I thought you'd probably know." He paused. "Not that you've ever had a one-night stand, but—" Pete could barely fight back a grin at the mortified expression on her face. "I won't go into all the details, but we—this gorgeous woman and I—ended up in the throes of passion and one thing led to another and—"

"I really don't need to hear this," Nora said, covering her ears with her hands.

"I think you do. How can you give advice if you don't know all the details? As I said, this is a delicate matter." He reached over her desk and took her hands, began toying with her fingers. The contact was electrifying, and he found himself lost in an idle contemplation of the pleasures he'd experienced by those hands, the intimate places they'd wandered on his body. "And you're so...delicate," he murmured, pressing his palm against hers, measuring its tiny size against his.

He glanced up to find her staring at him, lips slightly parted, her breath coming in short gasps. Pete twisted his fingers through hers. "You see, she left before I had a chance to get her name."

Nora blinked, then snatched her fingers away. "I don't see what difference her name makes."

"Well, it wouldn't usually. Except I want to see her again, which for me is a first. I've come to the realization that maybe I have some...deficiencies in my approach to women. And it's about time I work them out."

Nora shook her head, busying herself with a careful inventory of her pencils. "Deficiencies? Is that what you call them?"

"I'm sure you've heard about my reputation."

She nodded uneasily.

"Well, that's all in the past. I'm through with bar girls and bimbos. I have been for nearly a year. I've decided to take a more conservative approach to my social life. I want a woman with class, with refinement. A real lady. And the only way to get a lady is to become a gentleman. And that's why I've come to you."

"Me? You expect me to turn you into Prince Charming?"

He nodded. "Who better? Now, first, we need to deal with the problem of introductions—after the fact. How does a gentleman handle that?"

"After the—" She swallowed convulsively. "Well, you can't see her again! It wouldn't be proper. If a lady doesn't offer her name to a gentleman, then I think her intent is clear. She has no interest in seeing you again."

"That's not an option," Pete replied. "I *will* see her again." He rubbed his chin thoughtfully. "But I have to be ready. This isn't just any woman we're talking about. She's got class, sophistication. I can't make any mistakes."

Nora leveled her gaze on him. "She slept with you on the first date. You call that classy?"

Regret underlay her words, and Pete realized what

it had taken for Nora to admit as much. She was every inch the lady and took great pride in her propriety. That's what made their encounter so intriguing, so indelibly etched in his memory. The prissy little Prudence tossing aside all her inhibitions at the first touch of his hands on her body.

"I just need to figure out a way to go back to the beginning," he continued. "To start fresh. This is a woman I could... Well, it could be serious. But I need to woo her."

She scoffed, then shook her head in disgust. "Woo? Don't you think you should have put the woo *before* the woo-woo?" It was typical Prudence—concise, honest and dripping with sarcasm.

"And maybe you ought to loosen that bun a little bit, Prudence. You're sounding a bit judgmental."

She reached back and nervously toyed with the knot at her nape, then folded her hands primly in front of her and regarded him with a condescending eye.

"I made a mistake," Pete said, softening his tone. "And now I want to fix it. So, are you going to help me out here? Or are you going to slap my fingers with a ruler and make me wash blackboards for a month?"

Nora pushed to her feet and stalked to the door. "Do you want my advice? Well, here it is, Romeo. You've made your bed and...and now you're going to have to wash your own dirty laundry!" She flung the door open and swept her hand in front of her. "I have work to do. I'd like you to leave."

Pete stood and sauntered over to the door, pausing in front of her, standing just a little too close to be proper. Hell, he'd made love to the woman, he wasn't about to stand on formality. Her anger was palpable—and oh-so sexy. He even found her fractured clichés a turn-on. "If you change your mind, you know where to find me."

With that, he turned and walked out into the Bullpen. Two could play Prudence's little game, but he had no intention of playing fair. He wanted her back in his arms and back in his bed. And the only way to get her there was if *he* made all the rules.

A few seconds later, her office door slammed, causing most of the sportswriters to pop their heads over the walls of their cubicles in curiosity.

Pete grinned and shrugged. "I think she's really starting to like me."

NORA CURSED SOFTLY as she paced her office, wringing her hands until her fingers went numb. "He wants to see *her* again. Oh, good grief, what am I going to do?" She groaned and pressed her forehead to the wall, banging it a few times for good measure.

Mortification seized her brain, and she couldn't put a logical thought together. How would she ever extract herself from this awful mess? If he saw her again, certainly he'd recognize her! In the harsh light of day, even beneath the wig and heavy makeup, he'd know the truth: he'd made love to *her* last night—Nora Pierce!

Memories of their night together flooded back into her mind, each one more embarrassing than the next. She'd behaved like a wanton, a woman with absolutely no morals. And he thought she was classy? Good grief, what did that say about Pete Beckett? Yet, even through her mortification, she couldn't dislodge the tiny thrill she felt, and the corners of her mouth quirked up. "He wants to see *me* again." She giggled, then pressed her fingertips to her lips.

Since the moment she'd walked out his front door, she hadn't been able to put him out of her mind—the sensation of his hands and his lips on her body, the exquisite release she experienced with him deep inside her. She'd never been a passionate woman, but last night she'd tossed aside all propriety as though shrugging off an old coat.

"That wasn't me," she murmured, pushing aside emotion for logic. She had to put this unfortunate lapse behind her! But how was she supposed to do that with Pete Beckett strolling into her office whenever he felt the urge. And to come to her with such a tawdry request!

Did he actually expect her to help him drag this woman back into his bed? Sure, maybe he wanted another round or two of passionate lovemaking, but a leopard didn't just change his spots overnight. Men like Pete never changed. It was all about sex, sex, sex! "Love 'em and leave 'em," she muttered. "Wham, bam, thank you, ma'am. Why buy the cow when you can get the—"

Nora clenched her fists and screamed in frustration, then ripped off her trench coat and sunglasses. The game was supposed to be over, having ended the moment she walked out his front door! She'd never expected a second round.

At least this proved she'd been right—Pete didn't suspect she was the woman beneath the dark wig. As far as he knew, the woman he'd taken to the edge of ecstasy and beyond was still a stranger, a lover without a name.

Her mind returned to their time together and a slow shiver worked its way down her spine. She tried to look at things objectively. Was she really that exciting, so exciting that one night hadn't been enough? Or was there another reason he seemed so determined to see her again?

As she rubbed her forehead, a troublesome thought niggled. "Maybe he knows the truth," Nora murmured. "And he's just playing games with *me*." She brushed the notion aside. But no matter how much she wanted to ignore the possibility, she couldn't.

Added to all the other confusion and desire and mortification racing around in her head, this possibility was enough to make her brain overload. How could she keep it all straight? She'd thought a night with Pete would be simple—sex and nothing more; no strings, no regrets, no looking back. Just a quick end to her three-year dry spell. But less than twenty-four hours later, the simple act of making love had turned into a colossal headache.

"He can't possibly find me," Nora said, her words betraying none of the doubt she felt. "I'll burn the wig and the dress, and the evidence will be gone." She turned to her desk and grabbed a stack of file folders, then straightened them into a tidy pile. "I have nothing to worry about. And no one knows I was at that bar, except—" Her breath died in her throat.

The folders slipped from her hands as she reached for the phone. She punched in Ellie's extension three times before she got the sequence right, but there was no answer. Ellie would never tell, but what about Sam? If Sam knew she went to Vic's last night, it wouldn't be long before Pete knew. And if Pete knew, her secret wouldn't be a secret for a minute longer.

Nora dropped the phone back into the cradle, grabbed her coat and raced to the door. But when she yanked it open, she found her way blocked by the last person she expected to see. Celeste Pierce stood in front of her, her perfectly manicured hand raised to rap on the door.

"Mother!"

Celeste kissed the air beside both of Nora's cheeks before sweeping past her and primly taking a spot in one of the guest chairs. As always, she was decked out in her finest: Chanel suit straight from Paris, tasteful but expensive jewelry, and Italian shoes that she'd probably discard after six or seven outings. "Your father is very upset," she said, taking a recent copy of the *Herald* from beneath her arm and tossing it on Nora's desk.

Nora contemplated making a run for it. Her business with Ellie was far more important than listening to another of her mother's speeches. "Mother, I'm very busy this morning. I promise I'll call you tonight if you'll—"

"How are we supposed to handle this? All our friends know you're Prudence Trueheart. They all read your column, and I used to be proud. But lately, I'm just embarrassed. It's become so tacky. I can barely show my face at the Club."

"Mother, I know we've moved away from etiquette. But my publisher—"

"Your father thinks you should quit. He had his lawyers look at your contract, and they think they can get you out. You shouldn't have to lower yourself to such a level, Nora. Now, I know you value your independence, but until you find another job, you can move back home."

Nora took her mother's hand and gently pulled her up from the chair, then tucked the newspaper under her arm. "That's a very kind offer, Mother. And I promise to think about it. But right now, I have to get back to work." She led Celeste to the door and opened it, then gave her a quick peck on her cheek. "Thanks for stopping by, Mother. It's always a joy to see you."

Her mother stopped and turned to Nora. "Did you get my invitation for the opera benefit?"

Nora nodded, giving her another push.

"Mrs. Alexander asked if she could bring her son. He's a surgeon, you know. Quite successful and single. I'm going to seat him next to you."

"I'm bringing Stuart," Nora said, finally maneuvering her out the door and toward the elevator.

Celeste sighed. "He's nice enough. And he has perfect taste. But what do you really know about him? What about his family, his background?" She frowned as she studied Nora shrewdly. "Are you all right, dear? You look a little...flushed."

Nora clapped her hands to her cheeks. Was it still that obvious? Stuart had seen it last night, that well-satisfied look she'd worn. What if her mother recognized it, as well? She was thankful the elevator doors opened before she had to answer. She stepped inside with Celeste, pushed the button for the ground floor, then quickly stepped out. "Bye, Mother," she said, waving as the doors closed between them.

Knowing Celeste's penchant for interference, Nora felt downright lucky that the elevator had arrived quickly. How would she ever have explained her unseemly behavior? It just wasn't done, at least not by Celeste Pierce's sweet and sensible daughter.

Nora winced. But it had been done, and done well. Though she and Pete had been virtual strangers, the desire between them had been deep and stirring. She'd seen it in his eyes, the need to possess her. Her heart skipped, and Nora pressed her hand to her chest, trying to rid her mind of the image and the warmth that glowed deep inside her. She'd have to put these thoughts aside!

Rather than wait for the next elevator, Nora took off toward the stairs. The circulation department was on the tenth floor, and by the time she got there, she was gasping for breath. She found her friend bent over a computer terminal. Grabbing Ellie's arm, Nora hauled her to her office, pushed her inside and closed the door behind her, barring it against any other entry. "Did you tell anyone about last night?"

Ellie gave her a murderous look. "I came out of the ladies' room and you were gone," she said. "I was tempted to call the police—until I noticed that Pete Beckett had disappeared, as well. So, I put two and two together and came up with one incredible act of stupidity." Ellie clucked her tongue and shook her head. "You slept with him, didn't you."

Nora groaned. First Stuart, then her mother, and now Ellie. Did she have an account of last night's events tattooed on her forehead? Or was the guilty expression she wore proof enough? "Don't be ridiculous," Nora muttered. She didn't want to lie to Ellie, but telling her all the details out loud would make the night so real—make her feel so brazen.

Besides, Prudence Trueheart never condoned discussing intimate matters with friends. And Nora Pierce wasn't quite ready to deal with reality. She was still lost in the fantasy.

"We—we didn't sleep together," she said. "You'll be happy to know that I spent the night in my own bed. Alone." The last was added as an afterthought, but the explanation was weak and contrived.

"That's as far as it went? You left the bar and he took you home?"

Nora's life had become one long string of lies and deception, and it was getting harder and harder to keep it all straight. "Well, we did stop at his place."

"But you didn't sleep with him?"

Nora drew a shaky breath. "Not exactly. I mean, technically, there wasn't any sleeping involved."

Ellie's eyebrow arched in surprise and she waited for the rest of the explanation. When Nora refused to speak, Ellie shrugged. "Maybe I should ask Pete what happened," she suggested. "Do you think *he'd* kiss and tell?"

Nora flopped into a chair across from Ellie's desk. "All right. But if I tell you everything, you have to promise not to breathe a word to Sam." She toyed with a loose thread on her trench coat, waiting for the requisite promise. When Ellie finally nodded, the words came out in a rush, one long sentence without punctuation. "Prudence Trueheart had a one-night stand and it was of course incredible and all the rumors about Pete Beckett are completely true and after it was over I walked out without him ever realizing who I really was and now I can't get these thoughts of him out of my head!" Nora hit her forehead with the heel of her hand.

She drew a deep breath, then primly folded her hands on her lap and crossed her ankles. "So that's it. That's all I'm going to say. As far as I'm concerned, the matter is in the past." She closed her eyes and tried to regain her composure, but she couldn't catch her breath. "That is, it will be." She opened her eyes and gazed at Ellie. "The bar...Pete...the wig. Did you tell anyone?"

"No," Ellie said.

"Not even Sam?"

Ellie winced. "Well, I had to tell him where we were going. And he's the one who suggested Vic's, remember? He said the place was always crawling with single guys."

Nora reached out and grabbed Ellie by the shoulders, giving her a gentle shake. "You have to talk to Sam. You have to tell him that he can't mention this to Pete. Not a word."

"He'd never—"

"Promise me, Ellie. I don't care what you have to do, but Pete cannot know we were at Vic's last night. He'll figure it all out."

Ellie studied her soberly. "How could he not know it was you? The man's not stupid."

Nora pondered the question for a moment. True, Pete Beckett was far from stupid. He was warm and sexy and passionate and— "I don't know," she murmured. "But I'm glad he didn't. Maybe he was drunk, or maybe the wig was too much. Maybe he was too occupied with my body to even look at my face."

"Or maybe he knew and he just didn't let on?" Ellie suggested.

The breath froze in Nora's throat; the blood drained out of her cheeks. The thought had crossed her mind, but now it had crossed Ellie's, too! "You don't think..."

Ellie shrugged. "I can't form an opinion until I know more details." She slipped her arm through Nora's and kicked her feet up on the edge of the desk. "Let's hear them."

As they sat in the safe confines of Ellie's office, Nora carefully related the events of the night before, leaving out only the details that made her blush. By the time she'd finished, she'd convinced herself all over again that Pete Beckett had made love to a stranger. "If he knew it was me, Ellie, why would he ask me for help?"

"Help?"

"He wants to see this woman again and he asked that I—"

Ellie gasped. "What?"

"He really likes me...I mean, her. He thinks she's sexy and funny. And he wants me to turn him into a gentleman, the kind of man she'd—I mean, I'd—fall for."

Ellie shook her head. "Then you'd better tell him the truth, now. Before this all blows up in your face. When it comes to women, Pete Beckett always gets what he wants! If he wants you, Nora, he'll stop at nothing to get you."

"Pete Beckett does not want me! If he knew who he was with last night, he'd run in the opposite direction. Besides, I'm not going to tell him."

Ellie sighed in frustration. "Why not? You said you had a wonderful time. And he obviously did, too, if he wants another date. What's the problem?"

"That was her, and this is me! I am not the kind of woman who goes out to bars and picks up men and has incredibly hot sex with them."

"*Prudence* isn't that kind of woman. But you aren't Prudence, remember?" A smile curled Ellie's lips. "If you and Pete start dating, maybe you'll fall in love and get married. And then we can all go on vacations together and have our babies at the same—"

"I deceived him. I manipulated him. Men like him

don't play the fool gladly. If he ever learned the truth, he might be angry and take it out on me."

A long silence grew between them, the hum of Ellie's computer the only sound in the office. The complications of her actions seemed to grow larger by the minute. Why hadn't she listened to Ellie and left the bar? What had possessed her to suddenly begin living her life dangerously?

She hadn't been herself. Maybe it was the dress or the perfume or the champagne, but something had possessed her mind and her body, some bizarre force that had flipped a switch and turned her into a passionate, sensual being. But had it come from inside her? Or had it been Pete's promiscuous nature rubbing off on her?

"There is one way," Ellie finally said. "A way to make sure he never finds you—or her."

"How?"

"He wants your advice, so give it to him. There's nothing that says it has to be the right advice, is there?"

Nora considered the suggestion. It could work. She could provide the guidance Pete asked for, only she could guide him in the opposite direction, away from his mystery lady—and away from *her*. It would require spending more time with him, though that prospect wasn't at all disagreeable.

"I could do that," Nora murmured. "But you'd have to do your part. You have to keep Sam quiet. Promise me."

A wicked grin broke over Ellie's dour expression. "I'll keep him quiet under one condition—you lend me that wig. Sam has this thing about Xena, Warrior Princess, and if I stroll into the bedroom with that wig on, I can guarantee wild horses couldn't drag your secret out of him.''

Nora nodded. "You can have that wretched wig. I never want to see it again. I just want to put this whole experience in the past.''

Ellie stared at her for a few moments before reaching out to grab Nora's hand. "Don't be so quick to forget it, Nora. Passion like that doesn't come along every day. You two made a connection, and that's not something that goes away just because you want it to.''

Nora gave Ellie's hand a squeeze and nodded. Her friend was right. Nora had never had passion as intense as she'd shared with Pete Beckett. The memory of their lovemaking had been burned into her mind. But how long would it be before Pete's memories faded and he moved on to another conquest, a more beautiful, available woman? How long before she became just another in a long line of women with broken hearts?

A dagger of regret stabbed her, but she ignored the pain. She hadn't been the first woman in Pete Beckett's life and she certainly wouldn't be the last. It would serve her well to remember that.

PETE HADN'T SEEN HER LEAVE. Somehow, Nora had snuck out of her office without him noticing, without giving him another chance to set things right. He cursed, then snatched up the plastic golf club. Was this the way it would be? Pete Beckett, pining after a woman like some lovestruck fool, waiting with baited breath until he caught the briefest glimpse of her? Going all warm and soft inside every time he thought of her?

"Come on, Beckett. We don't have all day."

Pete looked up. The boys in the Bullpen were embroiled in yet another competition—this time, golf. He stared down at the plastic ball, then out at the small wastebasket that served as the first hole. Pushing thoughts of Nora from his mind, he took an easy, graceful swing. The plastic ball rose from the floor in a perfect arch, destined for the hole—just as a hazard named Nora Pierce stepped into the line of flight.

Everybody yelled "Fore!" But she obviously didn't know the meaning of the word. The small plastic ball hit her squarely on the forehead. This time she didn't cry out. Her lips moved with a silent oath as she sent him a withering glare.

"I'd like to talk to you," she muttered between clenched teeth. "In my office. Now." Nora turned on her heel and marched out of the Bullpen, accompanied by the abject apologies of all the sportswriters and photographers in attendance.

By the time she sat down, Pete was standing in the doorway, his shoulder braced against the doorjamb, a teasing grin on his face. "Should I get the burrito?"

"Sit," she said, rubbing her forehead.

"Aren't you going to say 'please'?"

Nora narrowed her eyes, and he did as he was asked.

"I've been thinking about your request for help," she said, watching him warily. "And I've decided that perhaps I can offer my expertise. It's not often a confirmed reprobate like you wants to change. But when it does happen, I should encourage the effort. I owe it to womankind."

"Thanks...I think."

"So, I'll answer your questions and dispense advice.

And I expect you to follow my advice. If you don't, then the deal's off."

Pete nodded in agreement. "Whatever you say, Ms. Trueheart."

Nora cleared her throat, then met his gaze directly. "My first bit of advice would be to forget this woman. She obviously doesn't want to be found. For all you know, she could be married or—"

"She's not married. She told me she wasn't."

"She could be lying."

"Lying? Just to get me into bed? I'm not sure womankind would appreciate that observation from Prudence Trueheart, guardian of feminine truth and honor."

Nora looked frustrated. "Are you going to listen to my advice or are you going to make snide comments?"

"I'm listening," he said, putting on a properly chastened demeanor.

"I suggest that you find another woman you're interested in, and we'll start from the beginning, without all the bedroom baggage. I'll teach you how to behave like a proper gentleman, how to court her, and you'll see that it isn't so difficult to be a nice guy."

"But I don't want another woman, I want *this* woman."

Nora ground her teeth. "How do you intend to find her? You don't even know her name!"

"I'll go back to the bar, ask around, see if anyone knows her. If that doesn't work, I'll run a personal ad or maybe hire a private detective. But I really don't think that will be necessary. Sooner or later, I think she'll come looking for me."

Nora arched her eyebrow and gave him a dubious look. "I doubt that."

Pete grinned. "You don't know what we shared. A woman just doesn't forget a night like that. In fact, I'm willing to bet that she'll come looking for me before I even make a move to look for her."

Nora held up her hand. "Putting your rather inflated ego aside for a moment, let me make one thing clear. I'll only do this for you under one condition— you don't try to contact this woman until I say you're ready. If you really want to be a gentleman, then we have some serious work to do. It may take time."

She got up from her desk and began to gather books from her credenza. When she'd scooped up a good twenty pounds, she dropped them in his lap. "Emily Post, Letitia Baldridge, Amy Vanderbilt. The patron saints of proper behavior. I want you to read these books carefully and be prepared to discuss what you've learned on Monday."

Pete flipped through the Emily Post, shaking his head. "I'm really more of a hands-on guy."

Nora sniffed. "Yes, you've told me."

"Can't you teach me what I need to know?"

"You want private lessons?" She appeared to consider his request, then sighed in resignation. "I suppose we could—"

"How about tonight? After work?"

"I can't. I've got to write my column tonight."

"Then tomorrow?"

"All right. We'll meet here in my office at noon. And remember, Mr. Beckett, a gentleman is always punctual."

Pete met her gaze, but didn't speak. An odd look suffused her expression, an emotion he couldn't quite read. Why couldn't she have been forgettable, like all the other women he'd dated? Why couldn't he put her aside and move on?

Finally, he held out his hand. "Then it's a deal?"

Nora hesitantly reached out and placed her fingers in his. But instead of shaking her hand, he drew it to his mouth and placed a kiss on her wrist. He allowed his lips to linger there too long—until she tugged her hand away.

"D-did you ever think the reason you want this woman so much is because she doesn't want you?" Nora asked.

Though the words were softly spoken, they cut deep, robbing him of a clever reply. He wasn't willing to believe she didn't care. There was something between them; he couldn't have been wrong. Pete slid the books off the desk, then stood. "Tomorrow. Noon."

Turning on his heel, he headed toward the door. As he closed it behind him, he saw Sam Kiley standing at the far side of the Bullpen, in the doorway to Pete's office. His friend watched him with a sly stare, eyes boring into Pete as he maneuvered through the Bullpen.

"Do you want to tell me what's going on between you two?" Sam asked, as Pete brushed by him and into his office.

"Nothing," Pete muttered, dropping the books on the desk.

Sam closed the office door behind, shutting out the noise from the Bullpen and adding a note of gravity to their conversation. He and Sam had been friends for a long time, but Pete wasn't sure he wanted to hear what his buddy had to say.

"Ellie just called me, frantic that I not tell you she and Nora went out to Vic's last night."

"Then why are we talking? Aren't you supposed to respect your wife's wishes? Isn't that written down in all the marriage manuals? Love, honor and obey."

"I know Ellie," Sam said, bracing his palms on the desk, as Pete sat down. "And if there's something going on between you and Nora, Ellie's going to put herself right in the middle of it. Being her faithful spouse, I'm going to get dragged along. I'd just like to know what I'm getting into."

"I'm not sure," Pete muttered, rubbing his forehead. "Do you believe in love at first sight?"

Sam blinked, caught off guard by the question. "I guess so."

"Did you fall in love with Ellie the first time you saw her?"

"What is all this about?" Sam demanded.

"I might be falling in love."

"You? With who?"

"With her. Prudence Trueheart. Nora Pierce. The woman in the dark wig who I seduced in my apartment."

"You're in love with three women?"

Pete shook his head and chuckled. "No, just one. They're all the same woman."

Confusion clouded Sam's expression. "I don't get it. And I'm not sure I want to."

"I've been having a few problems with it myself. See, women have always been so easy for me. Not the way you think, but because I've been able to figure out what they want. Yesterday, I beaned Prudence Trueheart with a baseball, then nursed her wounds. A few minutes later, I asked Nora Pierce to lunch and was disappointed when she refused the invitation. And last night, I made love to a stranger, the most passionate woman I'd ever met, and now I can't stop thinking about her."

"You made love to Prudence Trueheart?" Sam asked, confusion giving way to disbelief.

"Not exactly. Don't you see? She was different." Pete groaned, then pushed up from the desk and began to pace his office. "There's Nora, who's funny and bright and vulnerable. And there's Prudence, who drives me up the wall. And then there's this other woman, who just touches me and I go crazy with wanting her. And they're all the same woman. And I'm falling in love with each of them. Well, not with Prudence because she's a royal pain in the ass. But with the other two."

"Now I *know* I don't want to be in the middle of this," Sam said, jumping to his feet and hurrying to the door. "When you figure it all out, let me know. And if Ellie gives you any problems, just tell her to butt out."

The door closed behind Sam, leaving Pete to review what had just come out of his mouth. There was no way around it—he was falling in love with Nora Pierce. But was this really love, or had she been right? Was he simply coveting a woman he couldn't possibly have?

Pete snatched an autographed baseball from a shelf behind his desk. He tossed it up and caught it over and over again, banishing thoughts of her from his head. But nothing could rid his mind of the desire that nagged at his gut, the need that he couldn't ignore.

An image of them together, limbs twined, mouths

searching, flashed in his brain. He fumbled the ball, and it rolled beneath his desk. "Get a grip, Beckett," he muttered. "If you can fall *in* love that fast, then you can certainly fall *out* of love just as quickly."

5

"TABLE MANNERS," Nora said. "Nothing marks a gentleman more than impeccable table manners."

Pete had arrived at her office right at noon, surprising Nora with his punctuality. She'd assumed he was the kind of guy who liked to keep a girl waiting, liked to keep her...off balance. Nora straightened her spine and ignored the weakness in her knees. The moment he walked in, carrying a leather jacket, wearing a pair of jeans and a T-shirt that hugged his torso like a second skin, she felt it—the buzzing in her brain, the heat prickling her skin, the wild thumping in her chest. And the strange case of vertigo that made drawing breath a dizzying effort.

Though he dressed casually in the office, somehow his choice of Saturday-morning wardrobe made her uneasy. Etiquette usually dictated a conservative choice of apparel in a business situation. A T-shirt that revealed broad shoulders and an impossibly narrow waist was more appropriate for...pleasure.

Nora wanted their meeting to remain strictly business, so she'd chosen a tailored pantsuit and her usual prim blouse, a perfect choice for Prudence. The only concession to the weekend was her hair, freed from its knot to tumble around her shoulders. With cool efficiency, she pulled out the chair in front of her desk and motioned Pete to sit down. As he tossed his leather jacket over the back of a chair, he brushed by her, their bodies touching. A current sprang to life, stopping Nora's heart for an instant. She scolded herself. If she ever expected to put her night with Pete in the past, she'd have to ignore such unbidden reactions.

She'd just keep herself firmly in the image of Prudence, staid and conservative, painfully proper. Nora knew the moment she allowed herself to throw aside that image, she'd be lost. Nora Pierce was the kind of woman who jumped into bed with Pete Beckett. Prudence Trueheart wasn't.

Drawing on her resolve, she pasted a polite smile on her face. But the smile faded as she stood behind him, her attention caught by the fascinating way his hair curled at his nape. She'd touched his hair once before, but suddenly she couldn't recall the feel of it. Her hand reached out, the instinct to recall overwhelming. But then she snatched her fingers back, pressing them to her chest.

Perhaps this was a bad idea. Maybe even the worst idea she'd ever had! She'd already spent an entire night in sleepless contemplation of Pete Beckett's body, of the wicked things he'd done to her with that body. She'd hoped that thoughts of him would fade by degrees, that every night would get easier to bear. But, instead, she found herself caught in a tantalizing web of vivid memories—half-clothed bodies straining against each other, furtively whispered urgings, and aching need that raced through her bloodstream like liquid fire.

The memories came into sharper focus in his presence, and the remembered feel of his skin, the hard muscle of his shoulders, the smooth ripples of his belly made her fingers tingle. Fighting a tremor that rocked her body, Nora reached over his shoulder to straighten a wine goblet. The familiar scent of his cologne brought back another flood of images, and she closed her eyes and drew back.

She wasn't sure how long she stood there, swaying against the dizziness, attempting to regain her composure. But when she opened her eyes, she found Pete staring at her over his shoulder, a questioning arch to his eyebrow. "Well?"

"Table manners—" she repeated, the words catching in her throat. Spread out in front of him was a wide array of sterling silver flatware. In addition, she'd brought along china, crystal and a linen napkin. She pointed at the place setting. "I want you to study this very carefully."

"I know my manners," Pete said as he fiddled with an oyster fork. "Napkin on the lap, elbows off the table, and don't slurp the soup." He glanced over his shoulder again. "What is this? A tiny little fork for tiny little food?"

Nora snatched the oyster fork from his fingers and laid it back on the table in its proper place. "There's much more to table manners than the location of your elbows," she replied. "Say, for instance, you were invited to an...an alfresco dinner party at some swanky mansion in Sea Cliff."

Just the thought of arriving at one of her mother's charity events with Pete Beckett on her arm was enough to bring a blush to her cheeks. Of course, he'd look stunning in a tux, the starched white shirt in stark contrast to his tanned skin. And he'd charm every woman there, whether he had proper table manners or not.

"Al Fresco?" Pete muttered, interrupting her thoughts. "Didn't he used to play third base for the Dodgers?"

Nora groaned. All right, maybe his lack of sophistication would be painfully obvious. *"Alfresco* is not a—" She glanced down to find him grinning at her, a teasing glint in his eyes.

"I know what *alfresco* means," Pete said. "And what's there to know about a picnic? Avoid the beans, don't drink too much beer—and if the hamburgers are charred to a crisp, eat 'em, anyway."

"I don't mean a picnic," Nora said. "I mean a formal dinner party on a terrace overlooking the gardens. A black-tie event. When you sit down at the table, you'll be expected to know what these are for."

Pete placed his hands on either side of the place setting and sighed as he carefully examined the sterling silver utensils. "There's enough silverware here for ten people. Are we all expected to eat off the same plate, too?"

"I've laid it all out, but you'll rarely find a setting as elaborate as this. Except maybe at a formal state dinner with the president or queen of England. Still, it's good to know what each piece is."

Pete grimaced. "You're talking to a guy who eats ice cream out of the carton with a steak knife," he muttered.

"Now that you've taken your spot at the table, what do you do first?"

Frowning, Pete stared at the place setting, then snatched the folded linen napkin from beside the plate and spread it on his lap.

Nora smiled to herself and gave him an encouraging pat on the shoulder. She allowed her hand to rest there, to feel the hard muscle beneath the soft cotton of his T-shirt. Without thought, she smoothed her palm along the ridge of bone and sinew before snatching her fingers back. To hell with Prudence! The woman was beginning to drive Nora crazy with all her prissy rules and condescending comments.

"Very good," she said.

"I didn't do anything," Pete said.

"The—the napkin," she explained, her heart slamming in her chest. "That's the first thing. Once everyone is seated, you place your napkin on your lap. There may be food on the plate or wine in the glasses, but you don't touch anything until the hostess does." Nora pointed to the fork at Pete's far right and began. "The oyster fork rests in the soup spoon."

"I love oysters," Pete muttered dryly. "And I'm a big fan of soup. But where's the pork rind fork? An alfresco dinner is nothing without beer and pork rinds."

Nora sighed, secretly amused by his silliness. Prudence didn't tolerate silliness, but from a man like Pete, Nora found it very...stimulating. "This is important. You pick up the wrong fork, and everyone will know you're just trying to pass yourself off as a gentleman."

"When am I ever going to use this? I'm pretty sure this woman doesn't dine with the president or the queen."

"You never know," she said. "Now, let's continue. This is a marrow scoop. I think setting it is pretentious in this day and age, but you might see it." Nora reached around Pete's shoulders and picked up a piece from either side of his plate. "Now, the rest of the flatware works in pairs. Fish fork and knife. Entrée fork and knife. Main course fork and knife. Salad fork and knife. Fruit fork and knife.''

Before she realized what she was doing, she had her arms wrapped around him, her breasts pressed into his back. She drew a deep breath, the scent of his hair swirling through her brain. Slowly, Pete turned in his chair, his gaze dropping to her mouth. Nora froze, unsure of how to retreat gracefully—or whether she wanted to retreat at all. All she had to do was lean closer, ever so slightly, and brush her lips against his. Just let her instincts take control. She could do that, couldn't she? Just one kiss was all it would take, and he'd—

"Let's move on to salt and pepper," she said, clearing her throat and pulling away yet again.

"Oh, let's not," he said softly, his attention still focused on her mouth.

"There is a proper way to pass the salt and pepper."

Pete pushed out of his chair. As he stood, he slipped his hands around her waist. "And I'm sure it's quite fascinating, but I think we should blow off this boring party."

Nora blinked, acutely aware of the way his fingers splayed over her hips, the warmth seeping through her clothes to her skin. "Well, that's a little trickier," she said, swallowing hard. "You can't leave in the middle of a party. That would be an insult."

He leaned a bit closer, and for a moment, she thought he might kiss her. Should she close her eyes? Or continue to stare at him? Maybe if she put her hands on his chest, he would pull her into his embrace the same way he'd done that night, and they'd—

"Just tell me what to do," he said, his voice soft, persuasive.

"Well," she said, "you must pay attention to the signs."

"The signs?"

Nora nodded, dragging her gaze from his mouth to begin a detailed study of his chin. Such a strong chin, with a slight cleft, as if it had been chiseled from fine marble. "The rule of thumb is that you leave a half hour after the last food or drink is offered by the hostess. Not counting refills, of course."

He stared at her for a moment longer, then let his hands drop from her waist to her hips. "And what should I say?"

Just as she'd been aware of the warmth of his fingers through her clothes, she now felt the pull of his body, the heat that seemed to draw her nearer. They were nearly touching, hip to hip, when he stepped back.

Suddenly, the room seemed colder, the sky outside her window cloudier. Her pulse slowed to its normal rate, and she could finally draw a decent breath. "You should say, 'I've had a wonderful time, but I'm afraid I must be going.'"

"I have had a wonderful time," he said. "And I'm afraid *we* must be going." He grinned, grabbed her hand and pulled her toward the door. "This is no way to spend a sunny Saturday, with fish knives and oyster forks."

"Wh-what are you doing?" Nora stammered, digging in her heels to stop him.

He grabbed her purse from the top of her filing cabinet and hooked the strap over her shoulder. "I've learned enough for today. Now it's time for me to give you a few lessons."

As he dragged her out into the Bullpen and toward

the elevator, Nora thought about resisting. But even she knew whatever Pete had in store for her was infinitely more interesting and exciting than sterling flatware and crystal goblets and anything Prudence Trueheart might have to say. In Nora's opinion, oyster forks were endlessly boring.

"Where are we going?" she asked, as the elevator doors opened.

He smiled. "It's a surprise. One of my favorite alfresco activities. I promise, you'll have a good time."

NORA COULDN'T HELP but anticipate all the intriguing possibilities, as they wove through downtown San Francisco. Her mind had already conjured a gourmet picnic in a perfectly secluded spot, perhaps in Marin County. They'd nibble on food and sip wine, and before long, he'd kiss her. A gentle kiss at first, but then passion would ignite between them, as it had that one night, and he'd brush aside their lunch and push her back into the soft grass.

Of course, once he touched her, he'd forget all about the other woman. A kiss would be all it took to wash the memory of that one-night stand from his mind. They'd find a romantic bed-and-breakfast in Sausalito and spend an endless, passionate night together.

She settled back into the leather seat of his Mustang and smiled to herself, listening to the Eric Clapton song that blared from the speakers. It was only when the music stopped and Pete switched off the ignition that she bothered to notice where they were. They'd barely been in the car fifteen minutes, and this was definitely not Sausalito!

"We're at the stadium," she said, gazing out at the sparkling new structure from among a long row of cars. Pacific Bell Stadium had been built just blocks from the *Herald*'s office, set on a piece of land over-looking the China Basin. Though Nora had passed by numerous times, she'd never had reason to pay a visit.

Pete nodded, then pushed open his door. "It's not Candlestick," he said. "But I guess it will have to do." He circled around the car, opened her door and helped her out.

"But...we can't have a picnic here," Nora said, frowning. This was all wrong! Not at all like the picture in her head.

"Picnic? Who said anything about a picnic? We're here for the ball game."

Nora blinked. How could they possibly have an intimate alfresco meal in the midst of thousands of screaming fans? "If this is your idea of the perfect date, then—"

Pete laughed. "I'd never bring a date to a baseball game," he said as he slammed the car door. "I only watch baseball with friends."

"Oh," she said, the sound coming out on a sigh. "Is that what we are? Friends?" A stab of disappointment pierced her anticipation. Of course she was just a friend. How could Nora Pierce possibly compete with the woman he'd found so fascinating, so mysterious?

He stared at her for a moment, his gaze fixed to hers. She found no telltale emotion in his eyes, no clue to a deeper connection. Was it all in her mind, the electricity that crackled between them every time they touched? Was she just deluding herself into thinking there might be something there?

"Yeah," he finally said, nodding. "I think we are. We're definitely friends."

Pete grabbed her hand and pulled her along toward

the entrance. All her visions of soft kisses and passionate nights dissolved with every step. *Friends*. Buddies. The kind of pal a guy could take to a ball game. Why not? Isn't this exactly what she wanted, what she needed to put that night of passion firmly in the past?

When they got to the turnstile, Pete flashed his press badge at the attendant, and the uniformed man waved them past with the smile.

"I thought we'd be going somewhere to eat," Nora murmured.

"We can eat," Pete replied, moving toward a vendor's stand. "What do you want?"

The odor of spilled beer and roasting hot dogs assaulted her, and she wrinkled her nose. "I don't know anything about baseball. And you know my history with balls. Whenever I'm around a game with balls, I get hit in the head. Maybe I should just go—"

"You'll love this," he interrupted. "There's nothing like a beer and dog at the ballpark." Pete pushed a chili dog and a beer into her hands and grinned. "And since I'm not carrying a bat or a club or a stick, I think you'll be safe from incoming balls. If one comes your way, I promise to protect you." With that, he turned toward the ramp.

Nora had no choice but to follow him. She sniffed at the chili dog, and her stomach growled in response. She hadn't eaten a hot dog since... Nora frowned. She wasn't sure that she'd *ever* eaten a hot dog! Her mother had ordered the family cook to serve only the finest cuisine, so Nora was more familiar with caviar than with processed meat products.

They climbed several ramps, weaving in and out of fans, until Pete ushered her toward a wide opening. Her breath caught as she looked out over the lush ball diamond from high in the stands. The grass was so green it hurt her eyes, and the noise of the crowd sent a secret thrill through her. They slowly descended the aisle to two empty seats just above the rail.

"We can just sit anywhere?" she asked.

"These are my seats," Pete replied, holding her beer and chili dog, as she sat down. "Compliments of the *San Francisco Herald*. Best spot in the park to learn etiquette."

Nora raised her eyebrow. "Etiquette? Here?"

He sat down beside her. "Ballpark etiquette. I told you I could teach you a thing or two about manners. By the end of the night, you'll be a true-blue Giants fan."

His teasing grin warmed her blood, and she decided to indulge him. After all, they were friends, weren't they? And though the disappointment stung, perhaps it was for the best. Now she could put those wicked thoughts of him out of her mind, stop thinking about the passion they'd shared. Yes, this was for the best.

"I know nothing about baseball," Nora said. "My family isn't much for sports. My parents preferred more refined activities: the opera, the symphony, the ballet."

"Then I think we'll start our lesson with the chili dog," he said, arranging her meal on her lap, then doing the same for himself. "One can always tell a real fan by the way he balances a chili dog and a beer without spilling a drop. First, you pick up the dog with one hand, careful to hold it just right. Grab the beer with the other hand, then bite and sip. Bite and sip." He demonstrated with his little pinky extended, as if he were having tea with the Queen Mother.

Nora giggled as she copied his technique. But biting into a sloppy chili dog was beyond her capabilities, and after just one taste she had chili smeared across her chin and dribbling down the sleeve of her jacket.

"I can see we're going to have to work on your technique, rookie," Pete said softly. He reached out and wiped his thumb along her bottom lip. His touch sent a shiver racing through her body, the same way it had that night. Suddenly, the chili dog tasted like sand in her mouth. Her eyes followed his hand, as he licked the chili off his thumb.

For a moment, they didn't speak. Nora held her beer and chili dog, her hand frozen halfway to her mouth. If ever there were a perfect moment for a kiss, Nora knew this was it. She thought about taking another sloppy bite. Maybe he'd lick the chili off with his tongue this time. And maybe she could smear chili all over her body, and they could—

Nora dropped the chili dog back on her lap and took a long drink of her beer. She'd never been one for beer, but right now she would have gulped paint thinner to hide her uneasiness. He'd just made his feelings for her perfectly clear. They were friends! And a friend didn't just passionately kiss another friend at the drop of a hat, or the taste of a chili dog.

Before she realized it, she'd guzzled down half the glass of beer. To her mortification, a tiny burp slipped from her throat as she set the paper cup down. A flush of embarrassment followed, warming her cheeks. "Pardon me," she murmured, glancing around at the fans that surrounded her. "I'm so sorry. I don't know how that—"

"No," Pete said, his eyes wide with surprise. "That was quite good. I was about to make belching lesson number two. But since you've got it mastered, we'll move on.''

The thought of Prudence Trueheart belching suddenly seemed utterly ridiculous. Nora bit back a giggle, but she couldn't help herself and laughed out loud. ''Burping in public,'' she said. ''What would my readers say?''

Her little lapse in decorum broke the tension between them, and soon Nora had put her thoughts of kissing Pete Beckett aside and found herself enjoying his company. He taught her how to whistle with her little fingers stuck in her mouth, behavior that would horrify her mother. And he made her memorize the words to ''Take Me Out to the Ball Game,'' putting to use the endless singing lessons she'd endured as a child.

He also gave her tips on hassling the opposing batter and insulting the umpire's eyesight. She learned to score the game in a program he bought for her, and learned to wave a huge foam-rubber hand in time to the ''Mexican Hat Dance.'' By the seventh-inning stretch, she understood the subtleties of base-running and had come to greatly admire the backside of the Giants' first baseman.

Pete gave her a pair of binoculars he'd retrieved from the press box, and she watched the pitcher go through his windup. When she leaned back in her chair, she noticed that Pete had draped his arm across the back. As he sipped his beer, he distractedly rubbed her shoulder, his fingers tracing lazy circles on her skin through the silken fabric of her blouse. She was so caught up in the delicious sensations skittering up and down her arm that she didn't notice the foul ball.

It was only when everyone around her began to

shout and stand that her gaze caught the arc of the ball as it whistled through the air toward her. Nora screamed, dropped the binoculars, and covered her head with her arms. Her beer dropped to the ground and splattered up on her legs. She waited for the ball to hit her, anticipating the pain, but nothing happened. Seconds ticked by, and she gathered her courage and peeked up.

Pete held the baseball in his hand, then tossed it up in front of him. All around him, fans were slapping him on the back and congratulating him. "I told you, you'd be safe with me."

Nora let out a tightly held breath and took the ball from his outstretched hand. She winced when she saw the red welt on his palm. "Ouch! Does that hurt?"

Pete shook his head. "Nah, I'm tough. But you could always kiss it and make it better." The devilish twinkle in his eye told her he was teasing again. But she wasn't about to pass up the opportunity to give him a dose of his own medicine. Maybe she could make him want her as much as she wanted him. Nora took his hand and pressed a soft kiss into his palm. But when she looked up, his reaction took her by surprise. The smile had faded from his face, and he stared at her with what could only be described as...discomfort. She fought the impulse to apologize, then quickly dropped his hand, confused by his reaction.

The afternoon had been so perfect, the sun warm on her face, the companion beside her handsome and charming. For the first time in her life, she had felt completely comfortable with a man. For the first time, she had been able to be herself and not some uptight version of her professional persona. And she'd had to spoil it with her bumbling attempt at humor and her momentary lapse into lust.

She was thankful that the game ended after a short ninth inning. As everyone rose to leave, Nora took one last look at the field. She sighed and gathered up the souvenirs Pete had bought her. She'd thought that having Pete Beckett as a lover had been her ultimate fantasy come true. But there was more. Pete Beckett the friend was just as wonderful. As friends, there were no games between them, no lies to taint their newfound relationship. They'd found a fresh start, and she had no regrets—except that they'd never share another night of passion, never know each other in that wonderfully intimate way.

As they walked back to the car, Pete slipped his arm around her shoulders, and Nora felt herself stiffen. If they were going to be friends, she'd have to accept such casual contact without losing her composure. There would be times when Pete would hold her hand or press his palm into the small of her back, times when he might brush a strand of hair from her cheek and his finger might linger. She'd have to be prepared to hide the rush of pleasure she felt at his touch.

It wouldn't be easy.

It might even be impossible.

HE HAD THOUGHT ABOUT taking her to Vic's after the ball game, just to watch her reaction to familiar surroundings. But Pete didn't want anything to spoil the day. Instead, they drove across the Golden Gate Bridge to the little restaurant Nora suggested on Sausalito's quaint waterfront. There, they dined on seafood and enjoyed wine from her favorite Napa Valley vineyard. And throughout the meal, his mind drifted back to their one night together. Did she think about their encounter as much as he dwelled upon it?

At first, he'd believed that memories of their love-making would eventually fade—the taste of her mouth and the silken feel of her skin, the flood of sensation that raced through his body as he came inside her. But more and more, the memories had given way to a nagging need, a need to possess her again, the flesh and blood woman that haunted his dreams.

Spending time with her only made his desire more unbearable. Good Lord, he couldn't count the number of times he'd wanted to drag her into his arms and kiss her senseless, all the moments he thought about running his hands over the soft curves of her body. But would she react in the same way she had that night, with unbridled passion? Or would she draw away, repulsed?

He still couldn't reconcile the two women he knew—the wanton who cried out her pleasure in his arms, and the innocent who jumped every time he touched her. Somewhere beneath the surface, these two women became one, a notion that Pete found endlessly intriguing.

He parked the car near her house on Telegraph Hill, and they silently strolled along the narrow sidewalks until they reached her front steps. Nora's pale blond hair fluttered in the soft evening breeze and her lips were parted slightly.

"I had a wonderful time today," she murmured, her gaze cast downward.

He hooked his finger beneath her chin and forced her eyes to meet his. "But you're afraid you must be going?" he finished, recalling her etiquette lesson earlier that day.

With a winsome smile, she nodded, then turned to go inside. Pete grabbed her hand and pulled her to a stop. Had she been any other woman, he would have kissed her right then, long and soft, teasing at her lips with his tongue. He might even have picked her up and carried her up the stairs, through the door and into her bedroom.

But mixed with his overwhelming desire for Nora was a genuine confusion. He'd always been able to put his relationships with women in their proper perspective, to maintain absolute control. Women had a singular place in his life—and in his bed. With Nora Pierce, he was happy just to be with her, to stroll down a San Francisco street at twilight on a summer night, to hold her hand and to watch the waning sun paint her profile in a golden light.

"Why don't we walk?" he suggested, tucking her hand in the crook of his arm. They headed to the Filbert steps and slowly began to climb toward Coit Tower. On a landing, they stopped to catch their breath, and Pete glanced over at her. The soft light from a streetlamp illuminated her profile as she looked out toward the lights of the harbor and the East Bay beyond. "When will we have our next lesson?" he asked. "I could drop by tomorrow night. We could see a movie afterward, maybe?"

"I...don't think that would be a good idea," she said.

He couldn't read her expression, but her voice sounded cool and indifferent. "The movie? Or the dropping by? We could mix a little business with pleasure," he said.

Her eyes went wide but she still refused to look at him. "Pleasure?"

"What? Is there some rule of etiquette against that?"
The words came out dry and sarcastic, and he wanted
to take them back as soon as he uttered them.

She spun to face him, anger snapping in her eyes.
"What do you want from me?"

The question caught him off guard. In truth, he
wanted to run his fingers through her hair and press
her soft lips to his. He wanted to lose himself in the
sweet taste of her mouth, in the subtle scent of her.
And most of all, he wanted to take her back to his
condo and gently seduce her until she ached with the
same need that he did.

"I don't know what you mean," he muttered, angry
with himself.

"What is it about this woman?" she asked. "Why is
she so important to you? She's nothing more than a
stranger. One with loose morals, at that."

He couldn't state the obvious—that he found the
contradictions between the two Noras intriguing. That
he wanted both women in his life and in his bed.
"Don't you ever wonder whether you passed the love
of your life on the street? Or sat next to him on the
bus? Or maybe stood behind him at the grocery store?
I've known a lot of women, and I've come to the conclusion that meeting this woman might have been
fate."

"That's just your hormones talking," she said,
crossing her arms over her breasts.

He shook his head and leaned back against the railing, facing her. "I don't think so."

"Maybe you're just interested in the chase," she
countered.

"The chase?"

"The fact that she doesn't want you, that she ran

out, makes her more desirable. Would you feel the same way if she called you the next day and invited you to dinner with her parents?"

Pete considered the notion. In fact, the chase made absolutely no difference. This had all started out as a game, a little contest between the two of them, advance and retreat. Pete couldn't think of anything more wonderful than to have Nora want him as much as he wanted her. To have the freedom to touch her and kiss her and make love to her without reservation—and meet her parents, if necessary.

"See," she said. "The typical male reaction. Everything is fine when you do the chasing. But once she wants a commitment, you'll turn and run."

"You don't think much of me, do you?" Pete said.

His words stunned her, and for a moment, she didn't speak. Then her expression softened and she dropped her gaze to her hands, which clutched the railing. "I'm sorry. I guess I just wanted to understand."

"You don't think I have much of a chance, do you?" he said, praying that she'd answer in the affirmative. All he needed was a chance. He could make her see that the passion they shared didn't come along every day.

Nora shook her head. "I'm just not sure you can overcome your bad beginning. I mean, what are you going to do on your first date?" Weary with the conversation, she turned and started up the stairs.

He caught up with her and took her fingers in his, happy to be touching her again. "I don't know," he said. "What are we going to be doing?"

She froze, her foot poised on the next step, and

slowly turned to him. "On our first date?" she asked in a choked voice.

"No, on my first date with her. What would you suggest?"

"I don't have any suggestions," she said. This time she turned and walked down the steps. "I'm really tired. I'd like to go home now."

He caught up with her at the next landing and grabbed her arm. "This can be the next lesson. We can pretend this is a first date. You can tell me what to do."

"I don't date people I work with," Nora said.

"We're pretending. Let's pretend you're my mystery woman." He paused, waiting for her reaction, then saw a fleeting expression of unease cross her pretty features. "I've finally found you and I've asked you out on a date."

Nora had fixed her eyes on her shoes and was nervously shifting from one foot to the other.

"What do we do next?"

"I don't think we should...pretend that—"

"Come on," Pete said. "This will help. Now, is it all right if I hold your hand?"

She stared down at their fingers, twined together. "As a courtesy, if I need help getting out of a car. But normally, you'd take my elbow, then release it once the move was accomplished."

Pete untangled their fingers, then rubbed his palms together. "All right. Rule number one. No touching on the first date."

She nodded. "It might be considered too forward by some women, but then...perhaps it isn't a hard-and-fast rule."

Without her hand in his, he couldn't help but notice the look of disappointment in her eyes and the odd sense of loss he felt. He took her hand, turned her around, and they continued up the hill to the street that circled Coit Tower and the crest. They stopped at a spot that offered a breathtaking view of the sunset, the sky red behind the lights from the Golden Gate Bridge. In the east, a half-moon hung over the dusky blue horizon. Just visible in the growing darkness were the outlines of Alcatraz and Angel Island.

Without thinking, he slipped his hand around her waist and drew her closer, as they watched a ship chug beneath the bridge. Five minutes, and already he'd broken the first rule. No touching. But trying to keep his hands from Nora's body was like trying to stop breathing. It seemed so natural to feel her warmth beneath his palms, to create a point of contact between them that couldn't be broken.

"Now what?" he murmured, leaning near enough to enjoy the scent of her pale hair.

"Now we converse. You can comment on the scenery, or the weather, or tell me something about yourself. But don't get too personal."

"All right," Pete replied, glancing around. "Did you know this was the first place I visited when I moved to San Francisco? The day I moved into my place on Russian Hill, I took a walk and ended up here." Pete stared up at the bright white column of the Coit Tower, illuminated for the whole city to see. "I didn't know what it was, but I just kept walking until I got here."

"It's a memorial to the city's volunteer firefighters," Nora murmured. "Some people think it looks like the end of a fire hose."

Pete chuckled, cocking his head. "It does."

"It's named after Lillie Hitchcock Coit. When Lillie

was 17 years old, she ran away from a wedding party in all her bridesmaid's finery to chase after the fire engine from the Knickerbocker No. 5 company. They made her an honorary firefighter, and when she died a wealthy woman, she left the money for this tower. My father told me the story when I was little, and I wanted to be a fireman—I mean, firewoman—fireperson—for the longest time."

"But you became an etiquette columnist," he said.

"That's not what I set out to do. I wanted to work in an art museum. Instead, I help people with their problems."

"You're helping me," he said.

Nora smiled. "I'm helping you chase down a woman whose name you can't even remember just so you can seduce her again and then probably dump her. This isn't exactly rocket science or brain surgery."

They stopped and looked at an artist's work, spread out on the sidewalk, pretty watercolors of the view they'd just enjoyed. "What if she isn't the one?" Nora asked, after they'd moved on.

"I won't know until I see her again," Pete said.

A long silence grew between them, and by the time they circled the tower and headed back down the Filbert steps, the moon was high in the sky overhead and a faraway church bell rang the hour of eleven.

They stopped finally in front of her house, and Pete wasn't sure what to say or do. Saying "thank you" seemed such a cold and impersonal choice. Yet drawing her into his arms and kissing her wasn't an option.

"I had a nice time today," he finally ventured. He reached out and idly rubbed his hands along her arms. She was impossibly soft and tempting, and his gaze drifted over her face to her lips. "I should thank you for the help."

"It was...nothing," she murmured.

"Did I do all right?"

Nora blinked, then shifted uneasily. "You did fine," she said, forcing a smile and drawing away. "You were very charming and polite."

"So, if this was really our first date, then would you agree to a second?"

Nora nodded. "I'm sure I would."

"And what would we do?" Pete asked. "What would be the proper activity for a second date?"

Nora stared up at him in confusion. "I think you can figure that out on your own." She started up the stairs to the front porch, and he followed.

"What would you like to do? I mean, if you were her. And we were making plans for...tomorrow?"

"I don't know," she finally said. "Maybe you could take one of the boat tours of the Bay. Or you could have dinner atop the Bank of America building. Or you could—"

"Take a drive up to Napa?" he suggested. "I bet that would be romantic. We could stop at a few wineries, have dinner, drive back after the sun's gone down. What do you think?"

"I think Napa would be...perfect," Nora murmured distractedly, picking up her pace on the steps. "It would have to be a warm day. And you should rent a convertible. They're very romantic. And—and there should be music on the car radio. Tony Bennett or Frank Sinatra. They're both very romantic."

"Very romantic," he repeated, nodding in agreement. "I'll have to remember that."

When she reached the landing outside her apartment door, Nora stepped to the rail and fixed her gaze on a light far out in the East Bay. Pete bent over, bracing his elbows on the railing and linking his fingers together.

"I guess this is the end of our date," he said. He glanced up at her. "So, what comes next? What's the proper etiquette? Should I say, I'll call? Should I tell her I had a good time or should I play it cool? And what about a kiss?"

"A k-kiss?" Nora stammered.

"Too early?" He straightened and stepped in front of her. "I suppose it might be a little soon."

"No," Nora said. "It's not too soon. I think if you both had a...nice time, there's no harm. Sometimes you have to be...flexible. Rules don't always apply."

"If rules don't always apply, then maybe she'll kiss me," he murmured, staring down into her eyes.

For an instant, he sensed she wanted to make the first move. Pete waited, counting the seconds, watching the indecision in her eyes. A delicious blush colored her cheeks, and he knew without a doubt that if he kissed her, she wouldn't resist. Pete bent nearer, and she closed her eyes. Gently, exquisitely, he touched his mouth to hers. But this kiss was not a kiss between lovers. It became a first kiss, tentative yet intensely powerful.

With every ounce of willpower he possessed, Pete drew back. "How was that?" he asked. At that moment, it seemed as if the game had fallen away and he was looking into the eyes of his lover. But then indifference cooled her expression and she forced a smile.

"I think that was fine," she said.

"Just fine?"

Nora pulled her keys out of her purse, fumbling

with them for a moment before she had them firmly in her grasp. Her hands shook slightly, and he took a certain pleasure in the fact that the kiss had affected her as deeply as it had him. "I—I'm not the one to judge," she said, shoving the key into the lock. She glanced over her shoulder as she opened the door, then stepped inside. Pete made a move to follow her, but she quickly pushed the door shut, leaving just a narrow opening. "Thank you again for the ball game. And I'll see you at the office on Monday."

With that, the door closed with a dismissive *thud*. Pete stood on her front porch for a while, smiling to himself over the events of the day. Then he turned and jogged down the steps, whistling a cheery tune. All and all, the day had been a complete success. Nora was having more and more difficulty hiding her true feelings. Sooner or later, she'd have to end the game between them. And when she did, Pete would have exactly what he wanted.

6

"GOOD GRIEF! Who died?"

Nora peered around the giant bouquet on her desk and frowned at Ellie. She'd been expecting the Spanish Inquisition since she'd arrived, but a computer crash in Circulation had kept her friend busy for the entire morning. In truth, she'd hoped to hide the flowers before Ellie wandered downstairs. But trying to hide an arrangement so large in her tiny office was like hiding an elephant in a teacup.

"No one died," she said. In truth, the flowers should have been cause for celebration, if she only understood why they'd been sent. But the card tucked among the blossoms did not identify the motive, just the sender: Pete Beckett.

"Then what are the flowers for?" Ellie asked as she strolled into Nora's office and sat down. "A bouquet that big must mean you did something pretty spectacular." Ellie leaned over to sniff at a Casablanca lily. She closed her eyes as she inhaled and smiled dreamily. "Who sent them?"

"Maybe I bought them for myself," Nora said, straightening a stack of letters she'd been reading. "I thought the office needed a little cheer, so I—"

"Did I do well?"

They both looked up to find Pete standing in the doorway. Nora jumped up from her chair, scattering folders on the floor and ignoring the befuddled look in her friend's eyes. Her heart skipped a beat or two and her stomach fluttered. How was it that he looked more handsome every time she saw him? She felt like singing and dancing and giggling like a teenager. And at the same time, she felt like tearing her clothes off and throwing herself into his arms and begging him to take her, here and now. Could she feel more utterly confused by a man? She opened her mouth to speak—

"*You* sent these?" Ellie asked, her voice tinged with utter disbelief.

Pete grinned and nodded. "I picked them out myself. White lilies and red roses."

"They're beautiful," Nora said softly, reaching out to touch a velvety crimson rose.

Their gazes locked for a moment. "They reminded me of you," Pete said. "A study in contrast. Purity and passion."

Ellie coughed. Nora looked over at her friend and sent her a warning glare. If she could have shown her the door in any way that appeared remotely polite, she would have. At least then she'd be able to thank Pete in private.

He grinned at Ellie. "Smooth line, huh? I figured after the first date, flowers might be a nice touch. And the fact that I chose them myself is a plus. More romantic that way, right?"

"First date?" Ellie asked.

Nora's fingers froze on the petal of a lily. *Smooth line?* Was this just all more of his damn practice? She cursed herself inwardly. Once again, she'd been caught up in the silly fantasy, thinking that she was the one he really cared about. But this was all practice for that other woman! That hussy! That harlot!

"Very romantic," she murmured, snatching her fingers away and schooling her voice into cool detachment. "But you needn't have wasted your money. You could have just told me about your plans."

He shrugged. "Then you wouldn't have flowers to enjoy, would you? So, are you busy for lunch? I thought we could have another lesson. I need to figure out—"

"Lesson?" Ellie said.

"Lunch?" Nora said.

If she managed to learn one thing from their day at the ballpark, it was that she couldn't continue to spend time with Pete Beckett! Further lessons were out of the question. He'd just have to get his etiquette from books. "I can't," Nora said, quickly gathering the letters she'd spilled and shoving them in the file folder. "Ellie and I have plans, don't we, Ellie." She glanced at her watch, then circled around to the front of her desk, the folder tucked under her arm. "In fact, we're late. We have to go right now. Reservations. Popular restaurant. Hard to get." She grabbed her friend's arm and yanked her out of the chair, then hustled her past Pete and into the Bullpen. "Thanks again for the flowers," she called over her shoulder. "They're a very nice touch."

He was about to follow her, a frown furrowing his brow. But the elevator doors opened as if on command, and Nora stepped inside. When the doors closed behind them, she slumped back against the wall and closed her eyes.

"Let me get this straight," Ellie said. "You had a date with Pete Beckett. And he sent you flowers. Not just any flowers, but big, expensive flowers. These flowers reminded him of your passion and purity. You slept with him again, didn't you!"

"No," Nora said. "Weren't you listening? They weren't romantic flowers."

"Then what were they?"

"Practice flowers," she muttered. "To thank me for our practice date."

Ellie frowned, then rubbed her forehead. "I've only been married a year, but this must be something I missed out on. When I went on a date, it was a real date. I do recall practice kissing my pillow when I was twelve. And necking with the mirror when I was thirteen. But how does one have a 'practice date'?"

"After our etiquette lesson on Saturday, he took me to the ball game. Just as friends, because Pete Beckett doesn't take women to the ballpark with him."

"But he took you," Ellie said, her confusion obviously deepening. "Aren't you a woman?"

"Not to him. At least, not a woman he'd date. I'm just a friend, a buddy, a pal, according to him. Afterward, we pretended we were on a date. He was just practicing for—" Nora sniffed disdainfully "—*her*. I'm so sick of hearing about her! After all, what does she have that I don't have?" The elevator stopped and Nora strode out, not bothering to wait for Ellie's answer to her rhetorical question.

She must have something, for a man like Pete to be so obsessed. Could it just be about the sex? Because if Nora knew one thing, it was that she wasn't that great in bed. Or could Pete honestly believe that she—the other she—was his one and only? What had he said—*fate?* She stopped dead in her tracks. "I've got to stop

thinking of her as another person. She's *me!* I'm *her!''*
It was time to put an end to her schizophrenia.

The truth might have been an option the morning
after. Or even the afternoon after. But too much time,
too many opportunities for honesty, had passed. How
could she possibly explain herself now without
sounding deceitful and manipulative—and absolutely, certifiably insane?

She'd made a deal with the devil for an evening of
passion, and now she was paying the price. Pete was
in love with the wrong woman. And the only way she
might have a chance with him was if she got rid of that
other woman. She had to convince him the real Nora
Pierce had much more to offer him than a one-night
stand with a stranger.

And to that end, she'd come up with a plan. A plan
that just had to work.

Nora turned to explain to Ellie, but she found herself standing in the middle of the lobby. Alone. When
she glanced back at the elevator, she saw Ellie still inside, holding the door open. "Aren't you coming?"

"No!" Ellie said. "I am not getting involved."

With an impatient sigh, Nora strode back to the elevator, grabbed Ellie's arm and yanked her out, holding tight until the elevator door closed. "I'm not asking you to get involved. I'm just asking you to listen."

"I can't," Ellie whined, pressing her fingertips to
her temples and wincing.

"Why?"

"It's just that when I listen to you, I get a headache!"
She plopped down on a bench near a potted palm and
refused to move. "He's in love with you. Not the real
you, the other you, the you he's carrying a torch for.
But you don't want him to love that you. You want

him to love the other you, the you that's standing in front of me." Ellie drew a shaky breath. "And then there's the flowers. Which 'you' did he send them to?"

Nora opened her mouth, ready to snap out an answer. But she wasn't sure of her reply. *Which "you" did he send them to?* "Who cares? The point is, I have a plan to get rid of the other woman."

"So do I," Ellie said, shaking her head. "I'll just murder you and then I'll be rid of you both!"

"You can't murder me," Nora said with a smile, pulling Ellie to her feet. "Who'd be your best friend?"

"You know you're just getting yourself in deeper and deeper," Ellie warned. "If you're not careful, the only way out will be to move to Canada and take up a new identity. I say, you should ride that elevator back upstairs and tell him the truth."

"I could do that," Nora offered. "And I promise I will, if my plan doesn't work."

"What plan is that?"

"I'm going to make him fall in love with me. The real me. Come on, I'll tell you all the details."

Reluctantly, Ellie followed her. "We'd better find a noisy restaurant."

"Why?"

"So I can scream at you without causing a scene," Ellie yelled the minute they stepped out onto the street.

"We're not going to lunch. We're going to your house to get my wig."

Ellie stopped, clenching her fists. Had her friend been a child, Nora might have expected a full-blown tantrum, Ellie throwing herself down on the sidewalk, kicking and screaming.

"What are you planning?" she asked, her eyes narrowed, her gaze suspicious. "You—I mean, *she's* not going to see him again, is she?"

Nora shoved the file folder into Ellie's hands. "Read," she ordered.

Ellie stood in the middle of the sidewalk and scanned the reader letters Nora had so carefully assembled that morning. She wasn't going into this without doing her research. After all, she was Prudence Trueheart. She'd spent all night looking at her situation in an objective light and she'd developed a plan that was guaranteed to work, guaranteed to make Pete drop "the other woman" like a bad habit, leaving him free to pursue a relationship with a more suitable woman—like her.

"I don't get it," Ellie said. "What do these have to do with you? Or her?"

Nora sighed impatiently, then started down the street, Ellie hard on her heels. "It's simple. If I know anything about Pete Beckett, it's that he's a typical male. When faced with a demand for commitment, he'll run faster than a cheap pair of panty hose. Tomorrow night, I'm going to show up at his front door and inform him that we won't be—" she drew a deep breath "—intimate again until he makes a commitment. Pete Beckett won't want anything to do with me—I mean, her. He'll send her on her way, and she'll never have to see him again." Nora paused. "And I'll never have to hear about her again."

"And then he'll be free to fall in love with you," Ellie said. "And I do mean *you*."

Nora stood at the curb, waiting for the light to turn red. "That's the plan," she murmured. Though, now that she'd laid it all out in her head, she wasn't quite so confident that she'd be able to pull it off. She stared across the street and contemplated what she was about to do.

All this would have been so much simpler if she hadn't fallen in love with him, she mused. She could have put Pete out of her life and never had to wonder what might have been. But she couldn't do that, not now, no matter how hard she tried. For as surely as Pete Beckett was in love with the other woman, Nora Pierce was in love with Pete Beckett.

NORA STARED OUT the rain-spattered window of the car while she tried to gather her courage. Nervously, she reached up and adjusted the black wig. Her head itched and the bangs tickled her forehead, and she fought the urge to rip the wig off her head and toss it out into the gutter.

"Are you sure he's home?" Ellie asked.

Nora nodded, her gaze still fixed on Pete Beckett's front door. "I called twice before we left, and hung up. He answered."

"What are you going to say?"

"Just what we decided," Nora replied. "If he wants a relationship, I'm going to demand a commitment. I know it'll work. He'll send me packing."

Ellie gripped the steering wheel. "I'm going to wait out here for you."

"No," Nora replied, reaching for the door handle. "I'll take Muni home. There's a stop just down the street."

"But it's raining," Ellie said. "I can wait."

"I'll be all right," she assured her. She gave the wig a firm tug, then stepped from the car. Ellie gave her an encouraging wave, then drove off slowly, leaving Nora standing in the street. She looked up at the facade of Pete's condo. A light burned through the front blinds, and she saw a shadow pass by. Even a silhouette of Pete caused her pulse to quicken.

Nora wasn't sure how long she stood in the soft evening rain, gathering her courage and planning what she'd say. The damp had begun to seep through her clothes and drip down her face. If she was going to go, she had to go now, before she began to resemble a drowned rodent. Drawing a deep breath, she crossed the street and climbed the front steps to his door.

"I can't believe I'm doing this," she muttered, raising a shaky hand to the doorbell. The plan had seemed so simple and straightforward when she'd first worked it out. But now, frozen by indecision, she couldn't bring herself to put it all into action. "I should have my head examined." Balling her hand into a fist, she rapped sharply on the door, secretly praying that he wouldn't hear and that she'd have an excuse to leave.

But the door swung open almost instantly, surprising her so thoroughly that she didn't have time to turn and run. Pete stood in the doorway, the light shining from behind him. He wore a flannel shirt, unbuttoned, and a pair of baggy sweatpants that rode low on his hips. His feet were bare.

"It's you," he said. No surprise colored his voice, and Nora got the impression that he had fully expected her to show up at his door one day—though by his dress, not at that exact moment. Still, the open shirt was just enough to throw her off balance, to muddle her senses and confuse her intentions.

Her eyes followed a soft line of hair from his collarbone to his belly, then back up again. "Y-yes, it's me."

"I've been expecting you," he said, an enigmatic

smile twitching at his lips. He stepped aside, a silent invitation to enter. But Nora wasn't about to fall for that trick again.

"I just have a few things to say to you," she said. "I'll stay out here."

Pete sighed impatiently, then grabbed her arm and pulled her through the doorway. "It's raining. Don't be silly. Whatever you have to say you can say to me inside." He slammed the door behind her, and she jumped at the sound, as if her only route of escape had been irretrievably lost.

He circled to stand in front of her, his gaze never wavering, intent as a predatory beast who had sighted his prey. Nora took a step back, twisting her hands together in front of her. "I want you to know...that I'm not the kind of person who sleeps with just any man. And certainly not on the first...date."

"Good," Pete said, taking a step closer. "Because I'm not just any man." He reached out and slipped his arm around her waist. "Is that all?"

"N-no," Nora said. "There's more. I need to tell you that I'm not interested in a purely...sexual relationship. I'm looking for something more permanent. A commitment. Maybe even marriage."

She waited for his reaction, expecting him to draw away. She'd be lucky if the front door didn't hit her on the backside as he hustled her out. This would be the end of it, Nora knew. Quick and painless.

Her first hint that things had gone terribly wrong came when he nuzzled her neck. By the time his tantalizing trail of kisses had reached her earlobe, she concluded that he hadn't heard a word she'd said.

"I'm serious!"

"So am I," Pete murmured. "I guess we should start

with your family. If we're going to get married, I should meet your parents."

Married? Stunned, Nora twisted out of his embrace and retreated behind a nearby easy chair. "I don't think you understand. I want a man who will be there. A—a man who'll provide for me. A man who enjoys the things I do. Like—like shopping and decorating. Gourmet cooking and...sewing." She congratulated herself on quick thinking. No man enjoyed sewing!

He shrugged as he moved closer. "I'm sure over the next few months, I'll learn to love all the things you enjoy."

Frustrated, Nora held up her hand to stop his approach. "Wait! Are you saying that you're all right with this? The commitment, the parents? One woman, one man? Forever and ever?"

A smile curled the corners of his mouth, and Nora felt her knees go weak.

"I've been waiting for a woman like you all my life," he said.

"You really want to marry me?" she asked in disbelief.

"Actually, right now, I want something else much more." He reached out and tipped her chin up. "Right now, I want to kiss you. Very much."

This was definitely not going as planned! Nora scrambled for a way out, anything to keep his lips off hers. If she moved quickly, she might be able to get around him to the door. But Pete wasn't about to be deterred. He'd already captured her waist, and she watched as he bent nearer, anticipating the moment when his mouth would cover hers. Resigned to her fate, Nora realized that she'd just have to let him kiss her, just once. And then she'd go.

But like all her other plans, this one didn't work. His long, slow exploration of her lips sent waves of numbing sensation through her body. All thoughts of resistance faded, and she couldn't even muster the will to drag herself from his arms. She'd never get enough of him. The taste of his mouth was like the sweetest water after days in the desert. The feel of his hands on her face like a cool breeze.

Hesitantly, she touched his naked chest. Beneath her fingertips, his heart beat an even rhythm. Here was the man she wanted, so strong and determined to have her. What difference did it make that she wasn't really the woman he thought she was? She could be, for just one more night, couldn't she?

"No," Nora murmured, shaking her head and pushing him away. This was not right. Pete belonged with her, not with this woman she pretended to be! She had to leave, before she ruined everything. But then he reached out and took her hands, and all her resolve suddenly vanished.

What guarantee did she have that he'd fall in love with the real Nora? Maybe this was her only chance to experience passion again, passion with a man she truly loved. Emotion warred with common sense, befogging her mind until she wanted to scream out loud. Why did she have to need him so much?

"I—I have to go," Nora cried, turning for the door.

But a moment later, she was in his arms. He brought his mouth down on hers and kissed her, slowly and deeply, until her limbs went boneless and her body went limp. This was what she wanted, this was where she belonged.

"All right," Nora murmured against his mouth. "All right. I give up. Take me to bed."

Pete chuckled softly, his breath tickling her neck. "Not so fast, sweetheart. This time, we take it slow." His hands brushed over her ribs and lightly skimmed her breasts. One by one, he worked at the buttons of her blouse until the silk gaped open in the front. Lazily, he pushed the fabric aside and traced circles over the skin beneath her collarbone.

"I knew you'd come back," he murmured.

His touch had cast a spell over her. She felt as if she were being sucked into a whirlpool, drowning in a need that had slowly consumed her common sense and washed away her inhibition. She didn't have the strength to fight him, wasn't even sure she wanted to.

"How?" she asked, the word coming out like a sigh.

"You couldn't forget the night we spent together any more than I could."

"We were strangers," she said.

"But we're not strangers now. I know you. I know what you need." His words were soft, breathless. "I know what makes you burn and ache for me." He cupped her breast in his warm palm. "And what I don't know, I'm going to learn tonight. And the next night. And the night after that."

Nora wanted to believe there would be months and years of nights between them. But that would never happen—not if she didn't tell him the truth. Yet, if she told him the truth, he might never forgive her. He didn't want Nora Pierce! He wanted the fantasy, the sexy stranger who haunted his dreams and drove him wild with desire. She'd be that woman for one more night. She'd be his fantasy and accept the consequences.

"And what makes you burn?" she asked, her voice trembling slightly.

He rubbed his thumb over her nipple until it peaked beneath his caress. "All you have to do is touch me," he said.

And she did. She skimmed her hands along his shoulders, over his chest, down his belly to the waistband of his sweatpants. His warm skin prickled with gooseflesh, and Nora wondered at her ability to pique his need. Emboldened, she hooked a finger on the soft fabric and tugged it down over his hip. As if to match her, he smoothed his hand over her collarbone and pushed her blouse and jacket off her shoulder.

Each move in their little striptease drew them farther and farther from reality. Each caress enticed, slowly and methodically, until it seemed as if they'd entered a world where nothing existed except undeniable need and electrifying sensation. Nora thought they'd never rid themselves of their clothes. When she finally stood before him, naked, he stepped back and let his gaze drift along the length of her body.

"You're beautiful," he murmured. "I knew you would be."

Her cheeks warmed, not from embarrassment, but from overwhelming satisfaction. No matter what happened tonight and in the days that followed, she'd always remember the look in his eyes, the pleasure her body gave him. She reached out and took his hand, her gaze taking in his form, the wide shoulders and narrow waist, muscular legs. And his hard shaft, fully aroused.

"Take me to bed," she murmured, reaching down to touch him there before turning toward the bedroom.

With a low growl, Pete pulled her back, yanking her

against his body. Her breath caught as she felt his hot erection brand her flesh.

"Promise me," he said, his expression intense, unyielding.

Nora blinked, confused by his sudden change in mood. "What?"

"The games. They end right here. Right now. Before we walk into that bedroom."

Nora wasn't sure what he asked or what he wanted, but the desire that burned between them was no game now. It was real...powerful...undeniable. As his hands smoothed over her bare backside, she would have agreed to anything. She was beyond any attempt at resistance. She nodded, knowing full well that what they were about to do was wrong.

In one smooth move, he picked her up and wrapped her legs around his waist. As he walked toward the bedroom, she hugged him, pressing his face into her breasts, arching her back. And when they tumbled onto his bed and sank back into downy soft pillows, he didn't let go, trapping her beneath him with the weight of his body.

Nora wriggled until the tip of his shaft grazed her damp entrance. With a soft chuckle, Pete pushed up and shook his head. "Slow," he murmured, dipping his head to suck one nipple. "Slow." He turned his attention to the other nipple, swirling his tongue over the peak.

But he didn't stop there. With exquisite care, he began a languid exploration of her body with his lips and his tongue. Every inch of her skin became new territory to be lingered over and appreciated, tasted fully before moving on. When he reached her belly,

Nora held her breath, and when he delved lower, she let out a long sigh.

The shock of his tongue invading the most intimate spot on her body sent tremors through her limbs. Fire raced from her core to the very tips of her fingers and toes. With each flick of his tongue, she opened wider, rising to meet his warm mouth. She'd never felt such powerful pleasure, never had a man take her in such a bold way. Every nerve in her body vibrated, longing to end the torture, to share her climax with him.

Combing her hands through his hair, she called out his name. She wasn't sure how many times, but the sound of her own voice echoed in her head until she was certain she'd go mad. Slowly, the sound faded to a soft buzz, then a pinpoint of near silence. Every thought became centered on his lips and his tongue, and her body grew tense, hungering for release. She writhed beneath him.

One moment she was on the edge—and then she was gone. Wave after wave of ecstasy washed over her, battering her body until she was so spent she could take no more. But he didn't stop. Instead, he nibbled at the inside of her thighs, then the soft flesh behind her knees and the curve of her ankle.

The next time she opened her eyes, he was beside her and then above her. He gave her the condom, and she slipped it over his swollen shaft with trembling fingers. And then, he was inside her, his erection full and hard, filling her with heat. As they moved together, their limbs twined around each other's bodies until Nora couldn't tell where she began and he left off. She'd never felt such unadulterated joy, such utter emotion.

With every thrust, he surrendered a little more of

his soul, and when he pulled her on top of him, she looked down to find her emotions reflected in his own eyes. This wasn't sex anymore. Pete Beckett was making love to her, an act that was more than just physical. They touched each other, more deeply than either could have imagined. With a smile, Nora reached down to his mouth, dragging her thumb along his lip. He answered with a soft sigh, closing his eyes as he tried to maintain control.

But Nora wanted to possess him, to have him feel as vulnerable as she was. She moved on top of him, slowly at first and then faster. A few seconds later, he arched beneath her and cried out in pleasure. As she watched him come, Nora felt a single tear slip from the corner of her eye. She brushed it away, angry with herself for giving in to desire once again. That desire had become her weakness, the one thing she couldn't deny.

When he opened his eyes again, Nora slid off him and curled up against his warm body. Tears flooded her eyes, and she rolled over so he wouldn't see. With a ragged breath, he drew her against him, nestling her backside into the curve of his lap. His lips trailed over her shoulder and nuzzled her nape. "No more games," he murmured. "No more games."

He wrapped his arms around her and threw his leg over her hip, trapping her in his embrace. Perhaps, if she just closed her eyes and slept in his arms, everything would be okay in the morning. She'd wake up and everything would be set right.

But Nora knew that wasn't about to happen—not as long as she continued to deceive him. And not as long as Pete loved "the other woman." She'd tried so hard to imagine him loving *her*, looking into *her* eyes with the same desire. But Nora had never been an exciting or passionate woman. Without the disguise to hide behind, she was nothing more than ordinary.

An ordinary woman, who for a brief moment in time had found an extraordinary passion.

WHEN HE WOKE UP, her side of the bed was cold. Pete wasn't surprised, just disappointed. He'd assumed that the end of the game meant the end of her reticence. He threw his arm over his eyes to block the morning light that streamed through the bedroom window.

There had been a time when he'd been glad to go along with her little game. But he'd wanted it over, all the barriers between them torn down. Last night, he'd made love to Nora Pierce, and this morning, his feelings for her were stronger than ever. Slowly, the two women that had been Nora had merged in his mind—a friend he could trust and a lover who could disarm him with just a single touch of her hand.

Pete rolled over and pulled her pillow to his face. The scent of her perfume still clung to the sheets. He'd hoped that they'd wake up together, that they'd make love again with as much passion as they'd shared the night before. But Pete couldn't be impatient. As far as he was concerned, Nora was part of his life, part of the future, and there would be plenty of mornings in bed.

He smiled to himself, surprised by the conviction of his feelings. Love at first sight had always seemed such an impossibility. Desire at first sight was more understandable. But as Pete looked back over the past week, he realized that from the moment he'd looked into Nora's eyes, he'd been changed. And for the first time in his life, he'd opened himself to the possibility of love.

The feelings he had for her were stronger than any he'd felt before. Thoughts of her possessed his mind. He'd begun to live for the moments he could touch her and look into her eyes and listen to the sweet sound of her voice. With other women, he'd always been able to hold himself at a distance, but with Nora he didn't want to.

Hell, he'd even asked her to marry him, in a round-about way. Although the proposal had been merely part of the game, Pete didn't look upon the notion as impossible. The man who married Nora Pierce would be in for a lifetime of challenges. The days and nights would never be dull. Pete smiled to himself. He could be that man—loyal, strong, true. Hadn't he already proved that when it came to Nora he was willing to be anyone she wanted?

Pete ran his hand over the spot she'd warmed just hours before. Images of their lovemaking drifted through his mind, and he closed his eyes and savored each one. He'd been with his share of beautiful women, but Nora defied any attempt to quantify her beauty. It was as if her body had been made just for him. Her breasts for his hands, her lips for his kisses, the soft flesh of her thighs for his hips. Everything fit so—

His fingers came to rest on an unfamiliar object. For a moment, it didn't register, and then Pete realized that there was a small hairy animal in his bed. Cursing out loud, he bolted upright and scrambled off the bed, yanking the sheet along with him. There, where Nora's pillow had been, slept the creature. Pete watched it for a long moment, but it didn't move. It didn't look like any animal he'd ever seen. It was too small for a dog and too hairy for a cat. It was only then that he realized it wasn't an animal at all, but Nora's wig.

Pete laughed, rubbing his forehead. His heart still slammed against his chest as he crawled across the bed to grab the offending "creature." He held it up and smoothed the strands. Waking up with Nora's hair was not quite as satisfying as waking up with the rest of her. He rolled off the other side of the bed, dropped the wig on the nightstand and padded to the bathroom.

As the steam from the shower filled the bathroom, Pete stared at himself in the mirror, rubbing at the shadow of a beard. He forced a smile. By all rights, he should be happy. But things with Nora were far from settled. Perhaps she'd left the wig on purpose, as a sign to him that the game was well and truly over. But he still couldn't predict how she'd react to seeing him. Would they begin again, or would they pick up where they'd left off the night before?

Pete pulled back the shower curtain and stepped beneath the stinging water. Bracing his hands on the tile wall beneath the shower, he leaned forward and let the water pound on his neck and sluice down his back. For a while, he let his mind drift with thoughts of Nora. Nora naked in his arms. Nora sitting astride him, her color high, the dark wig tousled. Nora crying out her pleasure as he sank into her.

Other images teased at his brain. Nora holding his hand as they sat at the ballpark, the sun turning her pale hair to spun gold. Nora gazing into his eyes with that tempting mix of vulnerability and passion. He couldn't deny that she captivated him in every way.

Pete stayed in the shower until the water began to turn cold, then flipped off the faucets and ran his hands through his hair. He pushed aside the shower curtain and grabbed a towel. The air was cool from the open window high on the wall. Steam swirled around him, a haze almost too thick to see through. He stood in the middle of the bathroom, naked, letting the chill morning air dry his skin. Then he pulled the towel over his head and rubbed the water out of his hair—

"Look out, I'm going to fall!"

Pete yanked the towel from his face, then spun around at the sound of the voice, peering through the clouds of steam. "Nora?"

But there was no one in the bathroom with him. "Nora? Are you there?" He wrapped the towel around his waist, his chest and limbs still damp, then hurried back to the bedroom. But it was just as he'd left it, the bed linens still disheveled and Nora's wig sitting on the nightstand.

Slowly, he walked back to the bathroom and stepped in front of the mirror. "Damn, Beckett, you must have it bad for this woman. You're hearing voices. Her voice." He rubbed his face, then flipped on the hot water to fill the sink for shaving. As he spread the foam over his jawline, he stared at himself in the mirror. He could have sworn he'd heard her voice. Pete wasn't prone to hallucinations.

"Look out, I'm going to fall?" he repeated, drawing the razor from his ear to his chin. "What's that supposed to mean?" He rinsed the foam off the blade, frowning at his reflection. "If I'm hearing voices, it would help if they made sense."

Pete finished shaving, then went back to the bedroom to dress. As he pulled on his shirt, he glanced at the bed. He momentarily forgot the buttons on his shirt and, instead, made the bed, smoothing the comforter and fluffing the pillows before he was satisfied with the job.

There was every chance in the world that he and Nora would be spending another night in his bed. He smiled. For the first time in a long time, he allowed himself to feel optimistic. "Yeah," he murmured, thinking of the moment they'd be twisted together amid the bed linens. "It always pays to think positively."

7

"I WAS STANDING perfectly still! You're the one who started wobbling around."

Nora raced down the sidewalk, Stuart hard on her heels, then jumped into the front seat of Ellie's car. She slouched down, far enough so she could be hidden, yet still see Pete's condo through the front windshield of the car. Just moments before, she'd been perched on Stuart's shoulders, about to climb through the window of Pete Beckett's bathroom—that is, until she realized that Pete was still occupying his bathroom, naked, dripping water across the floor...in all his early-morning masculine glory.

"What's wrong?" Ellie asked.

"She tried to crawl through an open window!" Stuart replied, climbing into the back seat. "I thought we were going to ring the bell, but she dragged me along the side of the house and made me boost her up to an open window."

Nora swallowed hard, trying to slow her racing pulse and calm her nerves. She should have come on her own! But she didn't own a car, and carrying a ladder down Macondray Lane would have looked a little suspicious. She'd needed Ellie's wheels and Stuart's shoulders.

"This is why I had to get out of bed at seven in the

morning?" Ellie grumbled. "So you could pay a little early morning surprise visit?"

Stuart stretched his arms over his head and yawned. "A person shouldn't have to get up this early without coffee. She's a lot heavier than she looks. I could go for a nice cup of Kona with an almond biscotti. Regain my strength."

"Or a mocha latte," Ellie said, "with a glazed doughnut. The least she could have done for us was bring along some snacks."

The two had been complaining from the moment they got into the car together an hour before. After such a dismal first attempt, Nora was ready to send them both home and take care of her problem on her own. But, unfortunately, she needed them both now more than ever. "I'll buy you all the coffee you can drink, once we're finished," she said, her gaze fixed on a spot half a block east.

"I thought we were finished," Stuart asked. "I hoisted you up. Why didn't you crawl through the window?"

"He was there!" Nora said, slumping down even lower. She didn't bother to add that he was also naked. A shiver raced down her spine as the image reappeared in her mind. God, he was gorgeous. Like a Greek god. No wonder she was losing her mind. Their night together had addled her brain, her need for him now so intense that she couldn't think straight. That's why she'd left the wig behind, and why she was so determined to get it back.

"Isn't that the point?" Ellie asked. "Climbing through his window wouldn't be much of a surprise if he wasn't there."

"Who's he?" Stuart asked.

Nora held up her cell phone with a trembling hand. "I called and there was no answer. He wasn't supposed to be there!" She shoved the phone back into her purse. "He must have been in the shower when I called."

"Are you telling us you were trying to break in to Pete Beckett's apartment without him knowing?" Ellie asked.

Stuart frowned. "This is Pete Beckett's apartment?"

Ellie nodded. "I dropped her off here last night," she said, twisting around to face Stuart. "She was supposed to put some big plan into action, but she refuses to talk about it. Personally, I think she slept with him again."

Stuart leaned forward, bracing his arms between the two front seats. He scrutinized Nora's profile, but she refused to meet his gaze. "She does have that look."

Nora sighed. She'd seen the look that morning when she'd stood in front of her own bathroom mirror: the flushed complexion, the puffy lips, the eyes still glazed with memories of the night before. She was a well-satisfied woman, a woman aware of the power she could wield over the man she loved, and acutely aware of the power he held over her. Pete Beckett was in her blood, and there was nothing she could do to fight it.

She'd told herself their first night together had been a mistake. But that wasn't possible now, for their second night had seemed exquisitely perfect, so perfect that she didn't want to spoil it by discussing and dissecting his every move and her every reaction with her two best friends.

"Will you two stop talking about me as if I'm not here?" Nora snapped.

"Honey, you're not doing any talking," Stuart cried. "Why not us?"

A long silence descended over the car, and Nora held her breath, her pulse still pounding in her head. She hadn't anticipated seeing him that way! She'd barely grabbed hold of the windowsill and pulled herself up, before catching sight of him through the steamy interior of the bathroom.

The water had glistened on his smooth skin, dripping from his hair to run along his spine, past his narrow waist to his muscular backside. Her fingers had twitched as she imagined herself, wet and warm, stepping out of the shower behind him, gliding her palms over his hips, reaching around to caress his sex. She'd press her lips to his damp back, slowly lick off the droplets that clung to his skin, and then he'd turn in her embrace and the seduction would begin all over again.

Maybe they'd step back into the shower and make love beneath a torrent of warm water. Or maybe, he'd carry her back to the bed. Or maybe, he'd pick her up and perch her on the edge of the sink before he plunged inside her and brought her to a shattering climax.

That thought had caused her knees to go soft and her balance to waver. For a moment, she'd been sure she'd tumble down from her perch and land in a heap on top of poor Stuart. She'd called out a warning to him, before falling with a *thud* in the dirt beside him. Without another word, she'd scrambled to her feet, grabbed his hand and hightailed it back to the car.

"Shh! Look, there he is."

The trio stared out the windshield toward Pete's front door. From this distance, she could just barely make out his features, but that didn't stop a tiny thrill from racing through her. To her eye, he wasn't suffering any ill effects from waking up alone after another night of passion. His shower must have renewed his energy. It certainly had sent *her* pulse racing!

Pete jogged down the front steps, raking his hands through his damp hair. As he reached the sidewalk, he glanced down the street once. A tiny scream slipped from Nora's throat. "Get down," she cried. "He sees us!"

After a few moments, Ellie reached over and pulled her back up by the collar of her jacket. "We're all right. Look, he's pulling out of the garage now."

They all waited, convinced that logic would have him turn east, toward downtown. When he did, a collective sigh of relief reverberated through the car. "How close do you want me to follow him?" Ellie asked, turning on the ignition and gunning the engine.

"I don't want you to follow him at all. I'm going back inside. Come on, Stuart, I'll need another boost. Ellie, if anyone comes up the street, I want you to honk the horn. Pretend like you're picking someone up for work."

"Before we try this again, I think Stuart and I deserve an explanation," Ellie said. "After all, we are accomplices now."

"Yeah," Stuart added, stubbornly. "Why are you breaking into Pete Beckett's house?"

"I don't have much choice," Nora replied. "He didn't give me a key."

Ellie clucked her tongue. "That's not an answer."

Nora sighed. "All right. I left something in his—"

she was about to say *bedroom* "—house. Something I need to get back before he finds it."

Stuart leaned back in the seat and shook his head. "I'm not helping you through that window until you tell us both exactly what you're trying to steal."

A mutiny! Nora should have known she couldn't trust her two friends to mind their own business. "I left my wig somewhere inside," she finally said. "I fell asleep and it must have come off. I ran out in such a hurry, I didn't realize I wasn't wearing it until I got on Muni and saw my reflection in the window. If Pete finds that wig, I'm not sure what he'll think."

Ellie grinned smugly. "So you *did* sleep with him again."

"Yes!" Nora replied. "I just couldn't seem to help myself. And I'm sure you'll gloat over the fact that my plan to dump him didn't work. I tried to chase him off by asking for a commitment, and he asked me to marry him."

"*What?*" Ellie and Stuart cried in unison, sitting up straighter and turning to her, eyes wide with shock.

Nora waved her hand. "I'm sure it was just a tactic to get me into bed. Pete Beckett has no intention of marrying anyone, especially not her!" Nora shoved the passenger door open. "Once I get the wig back, this whole thing is over. I'm not going within fifty feet of Pete Beckett. I'm going to forget we ever slept together."

"I don't know how you've managed to turn a simple one-night stand into such a disaster," Ellie commented.

Nora bit her bottom lip. She was beginning to wonder the same thing herself. Her first blunder had been to assume he'd just forget her. Instead, he had come to her for help, hoping to find his mystery woman. Then she'd tried to sway him during their etiquette lesson, but he wouldn't listen to her advice. The decision to see him again last night had been pure stupidity. But when it came to Pete Beckett, she just couldn't think straight.

Now, she'd been reduced to breaking and entering. "This is the end of it," she said. "I promise."

She glanced back at Stuart and gave him an encouraging smile before they both stepped out of the car again. They hurried over to the narrow sidewalk that ran between Pete's house and his neighbor's. Though the area was bathed in early morning shadows, Nora knew a curious passerby might notice the two of them standing just yards from the sidewalk. To her relief, the small window to the bathroom was still open.

"Give me a boost," she ordered. "But this time, push me up a little higher." Stuart laced his fingers together, and she placed her foot in his hands. For a small man, Stuart was surprisingly strong, and she felt herself rise into the air. In a matter of seconds, she was staring into the confines of Pete's bathroom.

Towels were strewn across the floor and steam from his morning shower still hung in the air. "Higher," she whispered. "Just a bit more."

Before she knew it, she was nearly halfway through the tiny window, her legs dangling out behind her. Stuart had to let go of her feet, and she shimmied forward. But she'd either misjudged the size of the window or the size of her hips. There was no way to pull a leg through the opening, so she'd have no choice but to fall headlong into a pile of dirty laundry and wet towels.

"Would you like to tell me what you're doing?" came Stuart's muffled voice.

"I'm almost in!" she called. "Just a few more inches and I'll—"

She felt a hand clamp around her ankle and tug her in the opposite direction. "Stuart, stop! I can do this! I'm almost there." She spread her elbows, bracing them against the inside of the window to slow her descent. But Stuart just pulled harder. Finally, she could resist no longer, and she straightened her arms and slipped out of the window, crashing down on top of him.

With a colorful oath, Nora brushed her hair out of her eyes and glared at the man beneath her. But it wasn't Stuart she was sitting atop. It was one of San Francisco's finest—a policeman, his crisply pressed uniform covered with dirt, his silver badge glinting in the meager light between the houses, and his hat crushed beneath the heel of her shoe.

Nora scrambled to her feet. "Oh!" She reached out to help him up. "Oh, dear, I'm so sorry. I thought you were—" No, that wouldn't do! She couldn't implicate Stuart and Ellie in this disaster. Nora risked a look out to the street, and to her relief, Ellie's car was gone. Had Ellie honked to warn her? Perhaps she'd been so caught up in her post-shower fantasies of Pete that she hadn't heard.

Nora snatched up the officer's hat from the ground and brushed it off, frantically trying to restore its shape. "I realize this looks bad," she said. "But I know the person who lives here."

"Is that so?" the officer replied, his voice cold and indifferent to her apologetic smiles.

She glanced at the silver name tag above his pocket.

"Officer McNally." Nervously, she held out her hand. "It's a pleasure to meet you." The policeman stared down at her proffered hand, then fixed her with a stare that could have split granite. "I'm sorry," Nora said. "But it's not really breaking and entering if I know the person. Besides, I was only breaking and entering so I could steal—I mean, *recover* my own personal property."

"Uh-huh."

"I mean, you couldn't possibly suspect that I'd break the law. After all, I'm—" The words died in her throat. *Prudence Trueheart?* She weighed the benefits of telling Officer McNally her identity. Prudence Trueheart might serve her well to get out of a speeding ticket or a jaywalking citation. But breaking and entering was positively...criminal.

McNally pulled a pad from his back pocket and withdrew a pen. "Name?"

"Ah. Nora—Nora Pierce."

"What was it you were planning to steal, Ms. Pierce?"

Nora wondered if this was the correct moment to ask for an attorney. Would her answer be considered a confession? If she could only explain herself clearly, she was certain the officer would understand. "It was my wig. It's dark. Shoulder length." Nora placed her fingers beneath her ears. "Kind of a pageboy style with bangs. Really cute."

"And while you were stealing your wig, what else were you planning to go after. Cash? Jewelry? Computer equipment? Or maybe a television or two?"

"Of course not!" Nora said. "Why would I bring my television over here and then leave it? First of all, it's much too heavy for me to carry. And he already has a television. Not that we've ever watched it.'' Nora drew a ragged breath. "If you'll just let me go in and get my wig, I promise I'll be on my way. I just need a little boost.''

"I think we'd better go down to the station, ma'am," he countered. Handcuffs appeared from behind his back. "If you promise to cooperate, I won't use these.''

Grudgingly, Nora offered her wrists. What choice did she have? Perhaps if she just went along willingly, the officer would notice her impeccable behavior and good breeding and reconsider arresting her. She winced inwardly. What if he didn't? She'd be tossed in a cell with dangerous criminals, fingerprinted and photographed. They'd haul her before a judge and she'd—

"Oh, God," she murmured, "the press. This will be all over the paper." Nora grabbed the officer's sleeve. "I can't be arrested. I could lose my job."

The officer pulled open the back door of the squad car. "You should have thought of that before you climbed through that window, ma'am.''

PETE LEANED BACK in his chair and kicked his feet up on his desk. He tossed a baseball across his desk to Sam, then caught it when Sam threw it back. "It all happened so fast," he murmured, continuing their game of catch. "One minute she was at my front door, wearing that sexy wig, and the next, we were tearing each other's clothes off and rolling into bed." He nodded at the dark wig sitting in the center of his desk. "When I woke up, the wig was all that was left of her. She snuck out in the middle of the night. At least she waited until I was asleep this time."

Sam leaned forward and plucked at the dark hair. "I know that wig. Ellie brought it home the other night. I've got this thing for Xena, and she thought—well, we had a real nice time." He grinned. "So I guess you two straightened everything out?"

"The game is finally over," Pete replied, "although it came under bizarre conditions. Before we could be intimate again, she wanted a commitment. You know, meet the parents, date exclusively, think about marriage."

"What did you say?"

"I asked her to marry me," Pete said offhandedly.

Sam froze in midthrow. "You asked Prudence True-heart to be your wife?"

"Nora Pierce," Pete corrected. "I asked Nora Pierce."

"But you were just kidding, right?"

Pete shrugged. "It was still part of the game, so I guess I was. But the more I think about it, the more I realize I want this woman in my life. Permanently. On any terms. If it takes silly games and dark wigs to get us there, I'm willing to play along."

"What's with the wig?"

He'd wondered the same thing himself. Pete loved Nora's hair, the pale color that made her eyes look so incredibly blue. The silken strands that slipped through his fingers. And the sweet scent of flowers. "I don't know," Pete finally said. "When I see her, I plan to ask her." He stood up and walked to the door, looking out across the Bullpen to Nora's office. "She's late."

"Maybe she's sexually repressed," Sam postulated. "She can't—you know—unless she has the wig on."

"Believe me, she's not repressed," Pete said without

hesitation. He wandered back to his chair and sat down. "Even if she was a little repressed, it wouldn't make any difference. I love her the way she is."

They sat in silence for a long time, Sam nodding and Pete staring out into the Bullpen. Though he'd said the words before, he'd never realized the true impact of such a statement. He'd fallen in love with Nora Pierce.

He'd known her for little more than a week, but Pete was as sure of his feelings as he was of his own name. He wanted to spend hours talking to her, listening to the sound of her voice, watching her pretty face as she spoke, touching her at will. And when they weren't talking, he wanted to make love to her until they fell asleep in each other's arms.

"I know that sounds silly," Pete continued. "We barely know each other. And with my history, I should be—"

"It's not silly," Sam said. "I knew the minute I met Ellie, I'd marry her. It happens that way sometimes."

"What if Nora doesn't feel the same?" Pete asked. "You know, I've never been rejected by a woman."

"Never?" Sam asked, shocked and a bit awed by the admission.

"Not that I can remember."

They both considered the implications of Pete's history with women in silence. But the quiet was shattered an instant later when Ellie came racing through the door, breathless, her hair rumpled. Sam shot to his feet, a look of concern etched across his features.

Holding up her hand, Ellie struggled to speak. "Couldn't wait...elevator...took stairs...Nora...the window...and then there was a cop."

Pete stood and crossed his office. "What's wrong with Nora? Has she been in an accident?"

Ellie shook her head. "No accident. Arrested."

"Nora's been arrested?" Pete and Sam said in tandem. "When? Why?"

Ellie gulped, then nodded. "She was caught crawling into your bathroom window. The police are booking her for breaking and entering."

"Did she call you?" Sam asked.

"No, I was there," Ellie said. "I was driving the getaway car. And Stuart helped her in through the window. When we saw the cop, we took off. We left her—" she gulped in another breath "—dangling."

"Why would she break into my house?" Pete asked.

"She wanted...she had to get..." Ellie paused, frowning. She pressed her palm to her chest and gathered her composure. "I—I refuse to answer on the grounds that it may incriminate my best friend."

Pete snatched up the wig from his desk and waved it beneath Ellie's nose. "Was this what she was after?"

Biting her bottom lip, Ellie nodded.

"Why? She could have just called me. I would have brought it to the office."

"Then you know it's hers?" Ellie asked.

"Of course. Why wouldn't I? She wore it into my house last night and left without it."

Stunned, Ellie moved to sit down in one of Pete's chairs. "Oh, this is terrible. You knew it was her all along?"

He laughed sharply. "I would have had to be blind, deaf and completely stupid not to know."

Ellie moaned. "Oh, this is really terrible."

"That was all part of the game," Pete said. "She pretended to be a stranger, and I pretended I didn't know her."

"Except Nora was playing by a different set of rules.

She was under the impression you *didn't* know who
she really was. She thinks you're in love with this
other woman.''

"I'm in love with *her*," Pete said. "Both of her."

Ellie smiled. "Oh," she said with a sigh, "that's so
romantic."

Pete grabbed his jacket from a hook on the back of
the door. "I better go down and get her. I guess they
would have taken her to Central Station."

Ellie nodded. "And don't tell her I told you. She's
probably already mad that we left her behind."

He paused, his hand on the door. "She really
thought I didn't recognize her?" Pete shook his head,
bemused, then grabbed the wig and shoved it in his
jacket pocket. "Well, this should be interesting."

If he'd learned one thing about Nora Pierce, it was
to expect the unexpected. He hadn't expected her to
show up at his door last night. He hadn't expected her
to make love to him with such desire. And he hadn't
expected she'd end up in jail a day later. Pete grinned.
Maybe that's why he couldn't help falling in love with
her. Every day with Nora Pierce was an adventure.

"WHAT AM I DOING HERE?" Nora plopped down on a
cold, metal bench and stared morosely at the floor,
rubbing her temples with her fingers.

"First time in the slammer, honey?"

Nora nodded to the woman sitting next to her in the
holding cell. By her rather outrageous and provocative dress, Nora could only surmise that she was either a working girl or a woman with incredibly bizarre fashion sense. In truth, the small cell was filled
with ladies who chose to wear their underwear on the
outside. And she hadn't seen so much vinyl since the

weekend she shopped for new kitchen chairs. "This is all just a big misunderstanding," she explained.

The woman nodded sympathetically. "Men," she said. "Can't live with them, can't make a living without them."

Nora glanced up, anxious to correct her assumption. "Oh, no. I'm not...I mean...I didn't do...you know."

"Darlin', none of us did. We're all victims of big misunderstandings. But let me give you a little advice. When they ask about the money, just tell them you were collecting for charity."

Nora smiled, then went back to a careful study of her shoes. Had someone told her a few weeks back she'd be spending the day in a jail cell with a party of prostitutes she would have laughed. But this is where her "simple" one-night stand had led her—incarceration. And a possible criminal record. It was Pete's fault—his fault that he was so sweet and sexy and irresistible. His fault that he made her do such unlawful things. His fault that every time he touched her, she lost all control and gave in to desire.

"Men," Nora repeated, sighing.

"What's your name, darlin'? I'm Cherry Sweet. But my real name is Carol Ann Parker. I'm from Tulsa." She stared at Nora for a moment. "Are you sure this is your first time? You look awfully familiar. Did you ever work the Tenderloin? Or maybe for one of the escort services?"

"Oh, no," Nora said. "I haven't...I mean, I'm not—you know."

Carol Ann patted her hand. "None of us are. You just stick to that story, honey. With a face like yours, someone might just believe you." She paused, frowning. "You know, I never forget a face. It comes in handy in my line of work. You're not a cop, are you?"

Nora shook her head. "I'm sure we've never met."

A long silence grew between them. "Wait a second," Carol Ann said, her expression brightening. "I do know you. You're Prudence Trueheart! Hey girls, guess who we have here. It's Prudence Trueheart!"

The blood drained from Nora's face, and she shook her head vehemently. "No, no. That's not me. I just look like—"

"Prudence Trueheart!" another hooker cried. "I read her every day."

"I love your column!" a third girl said. "You look prettier than your picture."

"Do you make up those letters or are they from real people?"

Before she could protest any further, the entire population of the holding cell had gathered around her, cooing and squealing with delight. "All right," Nora said, holding her hands up and calming them all. "Shh! I—I am Prudence. And I'm here...undercover." Nora smiled inwardly. She'd never been quick on her feet, but she had to admit that the little white lie made more sense than the truth. "So you can't let anyone know I've been here, or it will blow my cover."

"So are you doing a special column about working girls?" Carol Ann asked. "All of us have plenty of great stories to tell. Like that time I had the salesman from Dubuque with the scuba gear fetish. Or when Lily had the banker from Duluth who liked to have clam dip rubbed all over his—"

The jail matron stepped up to the bars and whistled through her teeth. "Nora Pierce!"

Nora jumped up from the bench. "Yes, that's me.

I'm here." She hurried over to the door of the cell where the matron waited with a dour expression, grateful that she wouldn't have to hear any more stories. "I'm ready to go. Can I go now? Please tell me I can go."

The matron unlocked the door, then stepped aside. Nora turned back to find her cell mates waving enthusiastically. She returned the farewell, then hurried after the guard. The matron stopped outside a door marked Interrogation.

"Wait inside," she ordered.

The small room held only a table and three chairs. Bright light glared off the tile walls, which were completely void of decoration except for a sign that warned her not to smoke or spit on the floor. On one end, a mirrored window ran the width of the wall. She assumed someone was watching her, so she quickly took a seat and folded her hands in front of her, looking as contrite as possible.

Nora watched the clock above the door, counting off each minute. Fourteen had passed, and the contrite expression was beginning to cramp her face. To her relief, the door finally swung open during minute seventeen. She steeled herself for the coming interrogation, determined to prove her innocence. She opened her mouth, ready to offer her profuse apologies, but then snapped it shut.

"Wha— Oh, no. What are you doing here?"

In three long strides, Pete crossed the room. Nora rose on shaky legs. He circled the table and took her face between his palms, then kissed her. Softly, his mouth teased at hers and the kiss went way beyond mere greeting. She should have acted surprised or offended, but seeing him was such a relief...and kissing him felt so good.

"Are you all right?" he murmured, his breath warm on her lips. "Jeez, Nora, what were you thinking?"

She swallowed hard and tried to keep her hormones from racing away with her mind. "How did you know I was here?"

His gaze skimmed over her face, taking in every detail of her features as he spoke. "Ellie told me. She came tearing into the office, worried to death."

"Exactly what did she tell you?" Nora asked.

Pete reached into the pocket of his leather jacket. "She said you broke into my house looking for this." He held up her wig, then tossed it on the table beside her.

Nora's eyes went wide and she gasped. Had he thrown a rotting flounder into her lap, she couldn't have been more mortified. In a rush, the implications hit her full force. He knew the wig was hers. And if he knew the wig was hers, then he knew—oh, God, he knew everything! She tried to speak, but nothing came out.

"You left it under your pillow," Pete explained. "I brought it to work. If you were that worried about it, sweetheart, you could have called."

She swallowed hard, then let a soft moan slip from her lips. Her gaze darted between the wig and his face. "You—you knew?" she asked.

Pete smiled. "Of course I knew." He stared at her for several moments. "Ellie says you thought I didn't know. Nora, I've known since the moment I sat down next to you at Vic's. I just assumed you knew I knew. I thought that was all part of the game."

Her mind spun from the impact of his revelation.

He'd known all along! The first time he kissed her, the first time he made love to her, and the time after that. Every word, every caress, had been meant for her. He hadn't made love to some mystery woman, he'd made love to Nora Pierce.

"We had sex," she said. "Twice!"

"I know. And it was wonderful."

"You don't understand," she continued, shaking her head. "You had sex with *me*. Not her. Not some stranger you picked up in a bar, but me. How could you have sex with me?"

Pete raked his hands through his hair, his expression of concern giving way to confusion. "You were there, too. I think it's pretty clear why it happened."

"But you weren't supposed to know I was there!" she said, jumping to her feet. "Why didn't you say something?"

"The disguise, sex between strangers. It was... exciting. Besides, it was your game. You were supposed to tell me when it was over."

Nora groaned and buried her face in her hands. When she'd awakened in his bed earlier this morning, she hadn't thought things could get worse. Then she got arrested, and Nora was certain her life had reached its nadir. But this was beyond all imagination. Pete had known it was her all along. He'd touched her in such intimate places, he'd made her tremble with pleasure and ache with need. "I never meant for it to go so far," she murmured. She looked up at him. "It was just supposed to be a simple night out. I was going to flirt a little and then—" She drew a ragged breath. "This wasn't supposed to happen. It was foolish and wrong and...and I'm Prudence Trueheart! I should know better."

It had been so much easier to accept her actions when she was hiding behind the facade of Pete's mystery woman. But now she was forced to face those actions as her own. She'd turned against all common sense, everything she'd known to be right. "I'm not that woman," she murmured. "I'm not the woman you want."

Pete drew her into his embrace, but she pulled away, putting the table between them.

"You're exactly what I want," he said. "And what I need."

"No. I was just pretending." Without the wig and the makeup, she could never toss aside her inhibitions and give in to her passion. Without the disguise, she was just Nora Pierce, a stranger to real desire, a woman afraid to trust her heart to such an experienced man. "I th-think you should go," she said.

"I'm not going anywhere, Nora."

"We work together. It would be wrong for this to continue."

For a moment, he didn't speak, and then he turned away. She watched as he began to pace the room. "No," he said. "You are not going to blow this off just because we work together." He turned to face her. "How the hell could you think I didn't know? Your disguise wasn't that good." He crossed the room again and took her hands, lacing his fingers through hers. "The game is over. So what? That doesn't change the way I feel about you."

Nora shook her head. "You don't want me. You want her."

"There's no difference, Nora. Not anymore. You, her. It's the same person. You want this as much as I do. And if you want to hide behind propriety, then you're only fooling yourself."

"You don't understand." She drew a ragged breath. "I'm not exciting and mysterious and passionate." Her gaze rose to meet his, defiantly, vulnerably. "I'm Prudence Trueheart. I'm plain and ordinary. And someday you're going to realize that what we shared was just an illusion, a fantasy. And then you'll move on to someone else. Someone more exciting."

"Fantasies can become reality," he said. "They already have."

She glanced nervously at the door. "You'd better go," Nora said. "They're going to want to interrogate me soon."

He shook his head. "There won't be any interrogation or any charges filed. I explained everything to the officer that arrested you, and he said I could take you home. I think we better leave through the back door, though. When I came in, there were press gathering outside. There must be some big story going down."

"It wouldn't be right to be seen with you," she said, pulling her hands from his. "You should just go. Anything between us would be...unprofessional."

"Damn it, Nora, you're not going to throw this all away because we work together!" Pete swore. "That's the sorriest excuse I've ever heard. Hell, look at Sam and Ellie. They didn't let that stand in their way."

"I'm not Ellie. And you're certainly not Sam."

"What's that supposed to mean?"

"Sam wants Ellie for who she is. You want some fantasy, the excitement of a one-night stand, the mystery of an unknown woman. If we continued this, you'd be bored inside a week."

"Try me," Pete challenged.

"No," Nora said. "I don't want to trust you. And I know I can't trust myself when I'm around you. I—I think it would be best if we just stayed away from each other. I need time to think. Time to straighten out this mess."

Pete sighed. "All right. Take some time. But it's not going to change how you feel. I know you want me, Nora, as much as I want you." He picked up Nora's jacket and held it out. "Come on. I'll take you home. Maybe after a good night's sleep, you'll see things differently."

"This is my mistake," she murmured as she slipped her arms into the jacket. "I'm going to handle it on my own. I'll find my own way home."

His hands clutched her shoulders and he spun her around, forcing her gaze to meet his. "I'm damn tired of you referring to our time together as a mistake."

"Sex isn't love!" she cried. "I tell my readers that all the time. And you, of all people, should know that. Or did you love all those women you were with? All those women you can't even remember." Nora bent her head. "Just go," she said. "And leave me alone."

He stood silently for what felt to Nora like an eternity, then slowly let his hands drop away from her body. When he turned for the door, she nearly gave in and called his name, suddenly frightened without the warm touch of his hands. She fought hard to stop the impulse. It was so easy to lose herself with Pete, to forget who she was and what she represented. The woman beneath the dark wig was as much a stranger to her as she had been to Pete.

How could she have let passion and desire completely overwhelm her common sense? She'd done nothing to protect her heart. Every instinct told her that, in the end, Pete would hurt her. But he hadn't hurt her, she'd hurt herself by getting carried away by fantasy.

Yet, even through the pain and remorse, she couldn't stop herself from needing him or loving him. Day after day she'd counseled her readers on the very same thing: Stay true to yourself. And she'd done the exact opposite, turning herself into another woman for the sake of a man.

"I'm not her," Nora repeated, as the door shut behind Pete. "And I never will be."

She waited a few minutes before leaving the interrogation room. As she walked through the station house, no one seemed to note her presence. Had she truly been a criminal, escape might have been easy. But then, Nora didn't look like the typical criminal. When she reached the front doors, she pushed them open. But Nora wasn't prepared for the assault that followed.

Flashbulbs popped and microphones appeared beneath her nose. Somewhere nearby, a television camera whirred. She blinked, trying see through the dots that swam in front of her eyes. The reporters jostled and shoved until she was swallowed up by the crowd and unable to escape. At first, she assumed they were there for someone else. But then the first question was hurled her way.

"Ms. Pierce, why were you breaking into Pete Beckett's apartment?"

"Hey, Prudence, is it true you and Beckett are having a secret love affair?"

"Nora! Have you been charged with breaking and entering?"

"Are you pregnant with his child?"

Nora held up her hands to shield her face from the prying cameras and tried to push her way through the crowd. But the reporters wouldn't allow her to move. She cried out in fear and frustration, frantic for a way to escape.

Suddenly, Pete appeared, pushing aside the crowd as he led her to the safety of the sidewalk. The reporters surged after them, and Pete grabbed her hand and began to run. They ran nearly a block before Pete stopped beside his Mustang. He glanced over his shoulder, down the street, for their pursuers. Then he helped her inside and slammed the door.

A few moments later, he slipped behind the wheel and started the car. "I'm sorry," he said, pulling out into traffic and turning toward Telegraph Hill. "I saw a few reporters from the *Chronicle* out front, but I never imagined they'd be here for you."

"Thank you for—for saving me," she murmured.

He reached over and brushed a strand of hair from her cheek, letting his hand linger for a moment. Then he pulled the car back over the curb. "I know you don't have any reason to believe me, especially considering my rather dubious reputation with the ladies. You're right, I didn't love any of those women. I didn't know what love really was." He paused, then reached out and turned her gaze toward him. "Until I met you." Pete sighed. "I have to be honest, Nora. Given the chance, I wouldn't have done anything differently. So we began in an unconventional way—so what? That doesn't mean everything that follows is tainted."

She reached for the door handle. "I have to go," she said. "There won't be any parking near my house. I'll just walk from here."

Pete reached out and took her hand. He stared

down at her fingers, gently playing with them. Such an innocent gesture, yet Nora felt her resolve wavering. "Please, I—"

He placed his finger over her lips to stop her words. "Just listen," he said. "This may not be the right time or the right place. And you may not even believe me. But here goes." He drew a deep breath. "I'm in love with you, Nora. I don't know how or why it happened so quickly, but it happened. When I saw those reporters pushing you around, all I could think about was getting to your side and keeping you safe. I want to be there for you, always, forever, to watch over you, to make you happy."

"Pete, I—"

"I really don't care how you feel about me," he continued. "Well, maybe I do, but it's not going to change the way I feel about you. You can believe me or not, but I do love you. You. The woman sitting in front of me. The woman in the black wig. Prudence Trueheart. To me, they're all the same. They're all part of the woman I need."

Nora felt tears push at the corners of her eyes. She wanted to believe, wanted to surrender to her feelings. But she'd been operating on emotion for so long, she just couldn't trust herself anymore. She had to be alone, had to find the time to sort this all out and gain some perspective. "I—I really have to go."

With that, she hopped out of the car and hurried down the sidewalk. To her relief, Pete didn't try to follow her. Tears blurred her vision, and she stumbled once, nearly falling to her knees. When she finally stopped, her breath coming in gasps, she slipped into the shadows of a shop doorway.

She'd never meant for this to happen, never meant

to take Pete Beckett as her lover. But some irresistible force had drawn them together, and now he claimed he loved her. Nora pressed her palms to her face and shook her head. She should be shouting from the rooftops and dancing for joy, for there was no doubt in Nora's mind that she loved Pete Beckett in return.

But this wasn't a fantasy anymore. They weren't playing at passion. This was real. Pete Beckett claimed to love her. Yet one thought kept intruding, a warning spoken in Prudence's wary tones. Great sex just didn't turn into a deep and abiding love, as if by magic. *Love was supposed to come first.*

How many times had she seen through her readers the tragic consequences of a one-night stand? The dashed hopes and the angry recriminations. She'd never anticipated being caught in the middle of such a drama. But she was. And the experience made her emotions a mess of doubt and insecurity, and left her unable to distinguish desire from true feeling. Did she truly love him or just need him? And how could she possibly believe that Pete Beckett loved her?

More important, how could she stand it when he finally realized he didn't?

8

"I SIMPLY CAN'T BELIEVE THIS! My daughter arrested! The news plastered all over the papers!" Celeste Pierce paced back and forth across the width of Nora's tiny living room, her heels clicking on the hardwood floors. Nora watched from the sofa, dressed in her robe and fuzzy slippers, a mug of chamomile tea clutched in her hands.

She hadn't slept a wink the night before, and had called the office earlier that morning to say she'd be working at home. Nora rubbed her tired eyes, then picked up the morning edition of the *San Francisco Chronicle* from the coffee table. She hadn't been surprised by the coverage, considering the number of reporters who had gathered at the precinct. "It's not plastered all over. It's on page twelve. Three column inches and a small photo. No one will notice."

At least, not until the tabloids hit the stands, she added silently. After all, there was nothing more entertaining than the fall of someone as sanctimonious as Prudence Trueheart. No doubt, someone at the police station had made a tidy sum tipping off the press to her misery. The only bright spot was that the *Herald* wouldn't cover her disgrace.

She stared down at the picture. It had been snapped at the very instant Pete had appeared at her side and started to help her through the crowd. He was stand-

ing next to her, tall and strong, his arm wrapped pro-
tectively around her shoulders, his expression fierce.
Her face was partially hidden against his chest, but it
was apparent that she was the subject of the photo.

Nora ran her finger over Pete's image, smiling inwardly. She'd spent all last night thinking about what
he'd said, trying to believe it might be true. Pete Beckett loved her. Everytime the notion crossed her mind,
a tiny surge of hope shot through her. But then her
common sense doused the excitement, and she'd tell
herself that he couldn't possibly know how he really
felt.

He was still caught up in the mystery, the forbidden
pleasures of sex with a stranger. A mysterious, passionate, uninhibited stranger. Nora frowned, a slow
realization sinking into her tired brain. He'd known
her identity all along, from the moment he'd sat down
beside her at Vic's. Isn't that what he'd claimed? So he
really hadn't made love to a stranger, had he? He'd
just *pretended* to make love to a stranger.

She brushed the thought aside. "It'll all blow over,"
Nora said, placing the paper on the coffee table. What
good would it do to get caught up in another round of
indecision and rationalizations? She'd made up her
mind. Trying to forge a relationship from a two-night
stand was an impossible task. If she'd learned anything during her time as Prudence Trueheart, she
knew that sex before love could only result in heart-
break.

Celeste fanned herself with her pocketbook and
pressed her perfectly manicured hand to her chest.
"I've been answering the phone all morning. You
must know that your behavior reflects very badly on
your father and me. This could ruin us socially, Nora.

We'll be shunned at the Club. And—and people will refuse to attend my opera benefit. We're parents of a...criminal!"

Nora groaned, then grabbed a pillow from the sofa and hugged it to her body. "Please, don't you think you're being a little overdramatic? It was just a little breaking and entering. And the charges were dropped. They didn't even fingerprint me."

"If that's all it was, why did the *Chronicle* print the story?"

"Because I'm Prudence Trueheart. Even the merest hint of improper conduct is considered news. Besides, they've lost circulation to the *Herald,* and I suppose they think I'm partially to blame. Maybe they're out to ruin me."

She narrowed her eyes. "I knew this job was trouble the moment you took it! Journalism. What kind of profession is that for a well-bred lady? And furthermore, what ever possessed you to break into a man's house? Is this the kind of behavior that's condoned by the *Herald?* I thought I brought you up better than that."

"I wasn't really breaking in, I was just retrieving my property. Once everything was explained—"

"Property? What property could you have left behind in a stranger's apartment? And who is this Pete Beckett, this man in the photo with you?"

"He's just a man," Nora murmured, her thoughts drifting back to Pete once again. If only she believed in love at first sight. The notion went against every ounce of her practical nature. But if Pete had really fallen in love with her the moment he first touched her, then what they shared that first night wasn't technically sex before love, was it?

"Stop it!" she muttered, pressing her fingers to her temples and trying to banish his image from her mind.

"I will not stop," Celeste countered. "I'm your mother. I have—"

Nora sighed. "I wasn't talking to you. I was talking to myself."

Celeste arched her eyebrow. "Well? Who is this man?"

Why bother to hide it? Nora mused. Maybe it was time Celeste Pierce realized her daughter had a life. She had needs and desires, passions. And how she managed to satisfy those needs was entirely up to her!

"Actually, Mother, I spent the night with him. He didn't know it was me, at least I didn't think he did. I was wearing a disguise—a wig, which I left behind in his bed."

Her mother gasped, then sputtered. "Don't toy with me," she said. "Telling me outrageous stories will not soften the blow. I have no sense of humor, you know."

Nora took a slow sip of her tea, watching Celeste over the rim of the cup. "You should be happy, Mother. Heaven forbid they print the actual truth in the paper."

A knock sounded on her front door, and Nora slid off the sofa to answer it. No doubt, Stuart was anxious to render his opinion on the whole matter, and spend some time currying favor with his favorite socialite. Maybe the subject could be shifted from Nora's criminal activities to the decorations for Celeste's upcoming opera benefit. But it wasn't Stuart waiting on the other side of the door.

"Mr. Sterling!" Nora cried, tugging the front of her robe closed. She ran her fingers through her hair. "What are you doing here?"

"Ms. Pierce. I stopped by your office, and your assistant told me you'd be working at home today. All the better, since what I have to say involves a...delicate matter."

She stepped aside. "Please come in."

Her boss stayed rooted firmly on the other side of the threshold. "I think it would be better if I just got to the point."

Apprehension twisted her stomach into a knot. His expression, usually so upbeat and friendly, was icy and impersonal. "You saw the *Chronicle?*" she asked.

He nodded. "So have our lawyers. This morning they informed me that you're in breach of your contract. The morals clause strictly forbids any criminal activity."

"But I wasn't charged," Nora said. "It was all a misunderstanding."

"The kind of misunderstanding we could tolerate in Nora Pierce, but not in Prudence Trueheart. To that end, I'm afraid we must terminate your contract, effective immediately."

"You're firing me?" Nora asked, stunned.

Celeste wandered over to the door, smiling smugly. "You're firing her." The delight couldn't have been more evident in her voice. "Thank God! At least something good has come of this. Nora, aren't you going to introduce us?"

Nora glared at her mother. "Stay out of this!"

"We'll be running old columns until we hire your replacement," Sterling continued. "Of course, we won't say we fired you. That would only bring bad publicity. You've simply resigned. And if you go quietly, we'll give you a generous severance package—although we're not required to, considering the situation."

"But there were no charges," Nora repeated. "You can't do this."

"Oh, I'm sure he can," Celeste said, wrapping a sympathetic arm around Nora's shoulders. "Perhaps this is for the best, dear. You can give up this crackerbox of an apartment and move back home. You could go back to school. I'm sure your father could be convinced to finance a doctorate degree. Dr. Nora Pierce. A much more respectable choice than this journalism silliness."

"Mother, I'm twenty-eight years old! Far too old to live with my parents!"

Arthur Sterling forced a smile. "Well, I'm happy to see that we can be civil about this." He held out his hand to Celeste, who sent him a coy smile. "Mrs. Pierce, I'm sorry we couldn't have met under better circumstances."

"Mr. Sterling, do you enjoy opera?"

He frowned, confused by her question. "Why, yes. My wife and I have season tickets."

Celeste slipped her arm through his and led him out onto the porch. "I'm hosting a little benefit for the opera company and I'd be delighted if you'd come. I'll send a messenger over to your office with an invitation."

"That would be wonderful." Sterling turned and nodded at Nora. "Good luck with future endeavors, Ms. Pierce." With that, he descended the steps to the street.

Pleased with herself, Celeste strolled back to the door. "You never told me he was such a charming man, darling. And so handsome. I'd assume he has money. He does own the *Herald*, after all, although, he's probably new money. Ah, well, new money, old money. It's all green.''

Nora turned on her heel and strode back into the apartment. "I can't believe you, Mother! He came here to fire me, and you hit him up for a donation." She flopped down on the sofa, then drew a deep breath. Things just seemed to get worse and worse, like an avalanche gathering speed and threatening to bury her alive.

"I thought it would be so simple," she murmured. "Just one night of passion and my life would go on as it had before."

"What are you mumbling about?" Celeste sighed dramatically. "Nora, sit up straight. Bad posture is a sign of bad breeding. I do hope you don't slouch around like this at my party."

"I'm not coming to your party, Mother. I'll only embarrass you."

"You're coming," Celeste ordered. "You'd be conspicuous by your absence. And it's always better to face the gossips than give them a chance to talk even more. Besides, Constance and Stanford Alexander are bringing their son, Elliott, the surgeon. If you don't come, I'll have an uneven number. I can't have that at one of my dinner parties."

"There are going to be eighty people there, Mother. Who's going to count?"

Celeste picked up her purse from the coffee table, then bent over and gave Nora one of her chaste air kisses. "Get yourself a manicure," she said. "And have your hair done. I want you to look perfect for my party."

When the front door finally closed behind Celeste,

Nora let out a long groan. She lay down on the sofa, then curled into a little ball. "Now things can't possibly get any worse. I've been arrested and terminated and completely humiliated." Reaching out, she snatched the newspaper off the table, then turned on her back to gaze at the picture.

Maybe her life had completely crumbled since that fateful night at Vic's. But she'd also had more excitement in one week than she'd had in twenty-eight years of living. She'd known passion like she'd never known before and would never know again. She'd lived by her heart, done things that would once have been unthinkable. She'd broken the boundaries of the person she'd been, and was now irrevocably changed.

She stared at the image of Pete. A torrent of memories flooded her mind, vivid and intense. Nora closed her eyes, hugging the newspaper to her chest. She'd have to live with her memories—and her regrets. Without her job at the *Herald*, she wouldn't see Pete every day. In fact, she might never see him again.

An ache grew in the vicinity of her heart, and Nora held her breath, waiting for it to subside. This wasn't just an end to her short life on the edge. She should look at it as a new beginning, a chance to start fresh. What better way to put Pete Beckett in the past?

"I'll be all right," she said aloud. "I don't have to be Prudence anymore. I can just concentrate on me."

But the thought didn't give her a reprieve from her feelings. For Prudence Trueheart hadn't fallen in love with Pete Beckett. Nora Pierce had. And she'd have to be the one to fall out again.

PETE STOOD IN THE BULLPEN, staring across the cubicles at Nora's office door. She hadn't been to work in three days. He'd called her apartment at least five times each day, and the answering machine had dutifully recorded his messages. He might as well have been shouting into the wind for all the good his calls had done. Yesterday, he'd resorted to a personal visit, stopping by her apartment after work. But she was either out or not answering the door.

He'd hoped time and a little distance might make her see the error of her reasoning. Sure, maybe he had gone along with the game a bit too enthusiastically. But it was *her* game, *her* deception. He was the one who should be angry and upset!

Pete sighed, then pushed away from the cubicle and glanced up at the clock. It was almost time for the Friday golf match. He wandered down the hall to the lunchroom to get the plastic club and golf ball. As he entered, he noticed a crisp sheet of *Herald* stationery clinging to the refrigerator door.

He smiled, his heart beating a bit faster. So Nora *had* been in—at least long enough to put up one of her infamous etiquette memos. Pete stepped over and pulled the sheet off the refrigerator, then scanned the text. He expected a diatribe about empty coffeepots or dirty coffee mugs but, instead, found a carefully worded letter from Arthur Sterling: "With great regret...the resignation of Nora Pierce...effective Wednesday...wish her all the best."

Baffled, Pete slowly read the letter again, certain he'd been mistaken. Nora had resigned? All these days he'd been waiting, and she'd never intended to come back! Was this all because of what had happened between them? Did she feel so hurt that she couldn't face the prospect of seeing him every day at work?

Although he'd never claimed to understand Nora, he'd come to be able to read her feelings—or so he thought. Her eyes betrayed her emotions at every turn. From the moment he'd first touched her, it was there—a connection, a current that ran between them, drawing them nearer with every hour that passed. Damn it, he was in love and so was she! She just hadn't admitted it to herself yet.

"She can't do this," Pete muttered, crumpling the note in his fist. He strode out into the Bullpen, intending to grab his jacket and head over to Nora's apartment. But as he passed by her office, he noticed a light shining through the closed blinds.

He didn't bother to knock, just pushed the door open and stepped inside. Boxes littered the floor, and she stood behind the desk, shuffling through a stack of file folders. She stiffened slightly, the only acknowledgment she'd allow to his presence. He waited for her to look up, and when she didn't, he snapped, "What the hell is going on?"

She continued packing a small box with the personal possessions on her desk, examining each item before placing it inside. "I'm just gathering my things," she murmured.

"I can see that," Pete said. "I want to know why. Why did you resign?"

Nora smiled halfheartedly. "You saw the memo?"

Pete nodded. "Typical Sterling. Drop the bomb on Friday, and the smoke will be gone by Monday. What I don't understand is why he accepted your resignation. You've got a contract, don't you?"

She finally looked up at him, and the desperate vulnerability in her eyes cut him to the quick. "Read between the lines," she said. "I didn't resign. I was fired for breaching the morals clause in my contract. Sterling told me if I went quietly, he'd give me severance pay."

Her news struck him like a blow to the stomach. *Fired?* He wanted to fold her into his embrace, to smooth away all the hurt and whisper words of love into the soft curve of her neck. But he held his place, the desk an effective barrier between them. "He fired you because we made love?"

"In a roundabout way. He fired me because of the arrest, which wouldn't have happened if I hadn't gone to your apartment that night, which wouldn't have happened if I hadn't gone to Vic's. So I guess it all does lead back to that simple little one-night stand. Ironic, isn't it? Prudence Trueheart brought down by passion."

"You have to fight this," Pete said, bracing his hands on her desk. "This is unfair. I'm as much to blame as you. More to blame."

Nora shook her head. "But I signed the contract. I knew the terms." She paused in her packing. "It's not that bad. The past few months, I haven't really enjoyed writing the column. This might be a blessing in disguise. Now I can continue my studies in art history, in Paris or maybe Rome, somewhere they don't recognize me. I figure, if my life can change so drastically in just a week, who knows what can happen in a year?"

This time, nothing would stand in his way. In three long steps, he circled Nora's desk and took her by the shoulders. She might be able to put a positive spin on this, but the hell if *he* had to. "You aren't going to Paris or Rome." He took her face in his hands and kissed her, angrily and recklessly, frustrated by his inability to make her see reason. She didn't fight him, just melted slightly in his arms as if too exhausted to resist. Gently, his mouth tried to convince where his words had failed. "You shouldn't have to leave," he said softly.

"I want to leave."

"But I can help you."

"I think I've had all the help I can handle from you," Nora said with a dry laugh. She pulled out of his arms and went back to her packing, as if his kiss had had no effect on her. "You should be happy," she said. "Now you'll get that corner office."

"I don't give a damn about the office. I'm not going to let you walk away as if nothing happened between us."

"Us? There isn't an 'us.' Just a me and a you."

"That's not true."

Nora drew a deep breath and looked into his eyes. "Let's be honest, we've only *really* known each other a week. A week ago yesterday, you hit me with that baseball. How can there be an 'us' in just a week? An 'us' takes months, sometimes years." She carefully closed the top of a box. "And sometimes, there's never an 'us'."

"It has only been a week. Maybe, you're right. Maybe that's not long enough to fall in love. But if that's true, then it's also not long enough to give up on the possibility of love. Besides, I've been fascinated by you for ages, long before you showed up at Vic's. I just didn't know what to do about it."

She stared up at him, and for a moment, he thought he'd finally gotten through to her. But then a determined expression crossed her face, and she shook her head. "So many things have happened," Nora said.

"My life is in chaos. I'm not going to make any decisions about my future. Right now, I have to concentrate on getting through the next hour. And then the next day and the next week."

Even now, he could see the emotion in her eyes, the war between her mind and her heart. Without even thinking, he took her face between his hands and kissed her softly. "That's for the next hour," he murmured.

She shook her head, her gaze lowered. "Don't."

He kissed her again, this time more deeply, his mouth possessing hers completely. She didn't pull away, but he could taste her reticence and her indecision, could feel it in the way her hands fluttered across his chest. "That's for the next day."

He pulled back to find her eyes glazed with passion, her lips swollen. "Please, don't do this," she pleaded in a strangled voice. "Just go."

He kissed her once more, cradling her head in his hands and bending her back over her desk. The kiss was long and hot, tongues teasing at each other, fingers kneading flesh. Finally, he straightened. "And that's for next week." He drew a deep breath. "After that, I guess you'll be on your own."

With that, he turned and walked out of her office, closing the door softly behind him. Sam and his city desk boys had already gathered in the Bullpen. He strode over to his friend and clapped him on the back. "I'm not going to play today."

Sam glanced over at Nora's office. "She called Ellie last night and told her. Ellie was so upset, she cried all night. Man, I can't believe Sterling is doing this to her. Can't she fight it?"

"She doesn't want to. And I think that's my fault."

He headed toward his office, and Sam followed. They sat for a long time in silence, the sounds of the Bullpen drifting through the half-open door.

"I don't know what to do," Pete said finally. "I can't make her want me, even though I know she does. She's determined to put me out of her life. Jeez, it used to be so simple with women. But Nora is different. The longer I know her, the more complex this whole thing becomes. I can't get my mind around it. I'm not sure anymore what I want, except that I won't be happy unless I have her." Pete sighed. "Remember how I used to say that a woman can't be a friend and a lover at the same time?"

Sam nodded.

"Well, Nora is my friend *and* my lover, and suddenly, I don't want anyone else. She's the only woman I can imagine spending the rest of my life with. Does that sound stupid?"

Sam smiled sympathetically. "I always assumed when I finally found the woman of my dreams, it would be simple," he said. "Finding her was supposed to be the hard part. After that, it all would be smooth sailing."

"That's the way it was with you and Ellie, right? Love at first sight. Easy. Simple."

Sam shook his head. "Sure, it's exciting and exhilarating and more than you ever imagined. But it's never simple. It's like cooking. You've gone from the freezer to a full boil in a week. There's bound to be some steam. But sooner or later, you'll find a nice easy simmer."

"You're happy, aren't you?"

"Deliriously," Sam said with a smile. "But only because I've figured out the secret to a woman's mind."

Pete waited, then shook his head. "You're not going to tell me?"

"It's dangerous information," Sam teased. "I wouldn't want it to fall into the wrong hands."

"I think I can handle it."

"Don't take everything she says at face value," Sam began. "You have to look a little deeper to know what she's really thinking. Sometimes, all it takes is time for her real feelings to come to the surface. Don't force the issue with Nora. Stay out of her way until she's had a chance to consider her options. And then come back at her with all you've got."

"But she's talking about moving to Paris or Rome."

"Do you honestly believe she loves you?" Sam asked.

Pete nodded, so certain that he didn't even have to consider the question.

"Then she won't be moving to Paris or Rome," Sam said.

"How long should I wait?"

Sam stood up and walked to the door. "You'll know when the time is right. Trust your instincts."

Pete leaned back in his chair and stared at the door Sam had closed behind him. He'd never been a patient man. If he had been, he might have played along with Nora's game a little bit longer before he'd seduced her. He might have taken time to court her properly. That was the past, though, and nothing he could do would change it.

Now he had a chance to shape his future with Nora. He'd give her time to realize the true depth of her feelings for him, and when he approached her again, she'd be willing to listen. It sounded like a good plan, Pete mused. There was only one problem.

How the hell was he supposed to stay away from the woman he loved?

"GOOD HEAVENS!" Stuart cried. "By the look of this place, I'd say we got here just in time!" He pushed his way past Nora and strode into her apartment, followed closely by Ellie. Both of them carried large shopping bags in each hand, which they dropped on the floor at their feet.

Nora hurried to try to tidy things up a bit. She wore the same robe she'd been wearing the day Arthur Sterling had visited, but now the chenille had been stained with chocolate ice cream, hot mustard and a very fine Cabernet. The remains of her weeklong binge were scattered about the apartment: empty pizza boxes, ice-cream cartons, half-eaten bags of potato chips. A three-foot high stack of videos, already overdue at the video store, teetered near the television set, and a half-dozen magazines were open on the floor.

"Oh, sweetie," Ellie murmured. "Is this what you've been doing all week?"

Nora forced a smile. "It isn't how it seems. I mean, this isn't because of Pete Beckett. Not at all. I'm trying to eat so much that I get a terrible stomachache. Then I can call my mother and tell her that I can't come to her party, and it wouldn't be a lie. She always knows when I'm lying."

"I don't believe you," Ellie said. "This is because of Pete Beckett."

"No!" Nora insisted. She raced over to the coffee table and grabbed a jar of pickled herring. Then she held up a bag of chocolate chips and a bottle of root beer. "I'm almost there. I think this combination will probably do it. And if that doesn't work, I've got some *mu shu* pork coming from the Chinese restaurant down the block." She rubbed her tummy. "Really, it's starting to hurt. I swear."

Stuart braced his hands on his waist and surveyed the room. "Ellie, why don't you clean up this mess, and I'll make her an Alka Seltzer."

"I don't want an Alka Seltzer! That would ruin everything!"

Stuart took her by the arm and gently led her toward the bathroom. "Honey, once we get you cleaned up, you're going to be glad to have one. Then, we're all going to sit down and have a nice night. A little girls' night. We've brought facials and lotions, and Ellie and I are going to make you feel all pretty again."

"I don't want to feel pretty!" Nora said, digging her heels into the carpet.

She should have known better than to fight Stuart. He was relentless in getting his own way. By the time she finally emerged from the bathroom—freshly showered, dressed in a soft cotton robe, a towel wrapped around her wet hair—her apartment was spotless, with no trace of her junk food extravaganza in evidence. She had to admit, she did feel a lot better—except for the pangs in her tummy.

Nora sat down on the sofa and curled her feet beneath her, glancing back and forth between the stern expressions of Stuart and Ellie. No doubt, they were waiting for an explanation. Why had she closeted herself in her apartment for an entire week? Why had she embarked on a taste-fest of every known empty calorie? She didn't have any answers. All she knew was that her life had spun out of control and that massive quantities of chocolate ice cream seemed to make her feel better. "So, what are we supposed to do now? I'm not going to talk about Pete. You can forget that."

It had taken every ounce of her resolve to put him out of her mind over the past week. Time and time again, he'd intruded on her thoughts, images of him swimming in her brain until she thought she'd go mad. And now, with just a simple mention of his name, all the regrets came rushing back. Maybe it would be best to talk about it, to unburden her soul and admit her true feelings out loud.

Stuart sat down on the sofa and took her hand in his. "We didn't come here to talk about the past," he said. "It's girls' night, and we're here to have fun. Let's start with the makeovers."

"Makeovers?"

"Your mother's party is tomorrow night. You want to look your best, don't you?"

Nora shook her head. "I'm not going. I'm sorry, Stuart, I know you're looking forward to the party, but I just can't face all those people right now. There'll be the questions and the pity...and the secret delight in my downfall."

"Nonsense," Stuart said as he picked through one of the shopping bags. "We're going to that party. I wouldn't miss it for the world. First, the facials!"

Nora felt it best to go along with Ellie and Stuart. As long as they were kept busy with beauty treatments, they didn't have time to review the source of her misery. Whoever said "absence makes the heart grow fonder" had been very wise. By Monday, she'd convinced herself she might have been mistaken about the depth of her feelings for Pete. By Wednesday, she was certain she was still in love with him. And when she woke up this morning, she'd already started figuring out ways to accidentally run into him.

Stuart slapped a glob of icy-cold cream on her face, and all thoughts of Pete temporarily fled from her mind, driven away by the overpowering smell of rotten fruit. "What is that?" she asked, trying hard not to breathe through her nose.

"Count Rudolfo's Miracle Mask," Stuart said. "The European secret to luminous skin. You'd think at thirty dollars an ounce, they could make it smell better." He dipped another finger into the slimy green cream and smoothed it over Nora's chin.

Count Rudolfo, a chic cosmetics shop, was set amidst the classy boutiques around Union Square. Nora had walked by often, but always ignored the promises of "a whole new you" and claims of skin "irresistibly touchable."

"This is just what you need," Ellie said.

"'Tropical fruit extracts,'" Nora muttered, snatching up the box and reading the label. "'Pineapple, guava, mango.' Sounds very nutritious. If it doesn't work on my face, I can always spread a little on an English muffin." She readjusted the towel wrapped around her hair and closed her eyes.

"That's not what I mean," Ellie continued. "This will make you feel like a new woman. You'll want to go out and meet new men. Mark my words, in a few weeks you won't even remember what Pete Beckett looks like."

Nora opened her eyes and looked over at Ellie. "What if I don't want to meet new men?"

Stuart clucked his tongue. "You're not going to let your silly little affair with that man ruin your chances for future happiness, are you? After all, it was clear from the start that you two were all wrong for each other. Ellie should have warned you off."

"I did," Ellie said. "Remember that night in the bathroom at Vic's? I told you to stay away from him."

"He's a cad," Stuart said.

"A scoundrel," Ellie added.

Stuart nodded. "A low-down reprobate. Look at how he took advantage of you, Nora."

Nora tried to open her mouth, but the mask had begun to dry, rendering her face immobile. "He—he didn't really take advantage," Nora said, forming words with just her lips. "He thought it was all a game between us. I was the one who made the mistake, believing he didn't realize who I was. I can't really—"

"Blame him?" Stuart asked. "Of course, we'll blame him. It's all his fault. And if you never see him again in your life, it's all the better."

"Absolutely," Ellie said. "I don't care if he is Sam's best friend. I'm never going to talk to him again."

By now, the mask had hardened completely, making it impossible for Nora to speak clearly. She was left to listen to Ellie and Stuart illuminate the shortcomings of Pete Beckett in great detail, unable to offer any defense.

If her two best friends believed the relationship had been doomed from the start, how could she believe any different? Hadn't Ellie urged her to trust her heart? Hadn't Stuart encouraged her to believe in love? What had changed their minds?

"I think you should find a new boyfriend right away," Ellie said. "Just jump right back in. Didn't you tell me your mother wants to set you up with some surgeon?"

"Take this off!" Nora cried, pointing to the mask, now as hard as cement.

Stuart and Ellie frowned. "Ake iz aw?"

With a garbled curse, Nora stood up and strode to the bathroom. It took nearly five minutes to remove Count Rudolfo's concoction from her face and regain her powers of speech. But she had to admit that her face did look quite luminous and irresistibly touchable. Grabbing a clean towel, she walked back to the living room.

Ellie and Stuart were still engaged in a detailed account of Pete Beckett's flaws. Nora plopped down between them. "I know what you're trying to do. Reverse psychology. If you do everything you can to make me hate Pete Beckett, then I'll only love him more. Well, you needn't bother," Nora said. "I'm over him. I barely even think about him."

She'd never been much of a liar, but Nora prayed that her face betrayed nothing of her true feelings. She didn't want advice and she certainly didn't want pity. She'd made a mistake and now she was suffering the consequences.

"Maybe you two should leave," she murmured, dragging the towel from her damp hair. "I'm really tired and I haven't been sleeping well lately." She looked at Ellie, then Stuart. "Please. I promise, everything will be all right."

Her friends rose from the sofa and silently gathered the shopping bags. Nora walked them to the door, then kissed them both before showing them out. When she was finally alone again, the tears came unabated. Anger, frustration, heartache—emotions she hadn't even named yet—surged through her body, sapping her strength. Her back to the door, she slid down to the floor, clutching her knees to her chest.

If this was what it was like to lose at love, then she'd make a vow right now. Pete Beckett would be the first man she'd ever love. And the last.

9

"THAT'S NOT THE WAY to tie a bow tie!"

Pete stared at his reflection in the mirror above his dresser, plucking at his damp hair. Ellie Kiley stood behind him, carefully smoothing out the shoulders of his tuxedo. Stuart Anderson sat primly on the edge of Pete's bed. Until a few minutes ago, Stuart had been a stranger. But then he and Ellie had burst into Pete's condo with big plans for Pete's lonely Saturday night and precious little patience for questions or explanations.

They'd waved an invitation under his nose and had demanded to know if he owned his own tux. According to Ellie, Pete was about to attend a fancy party at Nora's parents' house and rescue her from the clutches of a lecherous surgeon. Black tie was required for the rescue mission, and if he played his cards right, they claimed he'd have Nora back by the end of the evening.

Over a week had passed since he'd seen Nora, and though he'd been tempted to call, Pete wasn't quite sure the moment was right. He'd been distracted by matters at the *Herald* and confused by his own feelings. By his account, he might have one, maybe two more shots to make this work, so he'd have to choose carefully. Cornering Nora at a fancy society affair was an opportunity he wasn't about to miss.

"How do you know Nora?" Pete asked, watching Stuart in the mirror.

"I'm her landlord," Stuart said. "And her best friend."

"*I'm* her best friend," Ellie countered. "Best friends are girls, not boys."

Stuart sniffed. "Well, I'm the one who boosted her up into his bathroom window."

"And I drove the getaway car," Ellie countered. "*And* I told Pete that Nora had been arrested so he could go bail her out."

Pete smoothed the bow tie around the collar of his shirt and attempted to tie it once more. "With friends like you two, I don't think Nora needs enemies," he teased. His little joke was met with icy glares. "Does Nora know you're scheming behind her back?"

"It's not a scheme," Ellie said. "Stuart can't go to the party and he feels badly, so he wants you to go in his place."

Pete glanced over at Stuart. From his sulky expression, it was obvious the poor guy hadn't given up his invitation willingly. But he seemed genuinely concerned for Nora's happiness, and Pete couldn't fault him for that.

"She thinks we hate you," Stuart said.

Pete wasn't about to ask if there was any truth to the statement. "I'm not so sure about crashing this party," he said, still working at the bow tie. "What if they just kick me out at the door?"

Ellie turned him around and smoothed the lapels of his jacket, then pushed his hands aside and began to work on the tie herself. "You're a charming man, Pete Beckett. I'm sure you'll find a way to get inside."

"And once you get inside, don't do anything stupid," Stuart warned. "Like blow your nose in your napkin or pick your teeth with your fork. I wouldn't want you to embarrass Nora."

Pete cursed softly as the collar of his shirt cut into his neck. "I'm not a rube. I know what fork to use. Fish fork, entrée fork, main course fork, salad fork, fruit fork. Wait until the hostess takes the first bite before you eat, and leave precisely one-half hour after the last offer of food or drink."

Both Ellie and Stuart looked stunned by his depth of knowledge. He was thankful that they didn't know he'd pretty much plumbed the entire etiquette ocean for those meager bits. Ellie finished with his bow tie and pronounced him fit to be seen. He took one last look in the mirror, then grabbed his keys from the top of his dresser and followed them both outside.

"Where is this party?" he asked.

"Sea Cliff," Ellie said. "I'm going to warn you that the house is a little...overwhelming. And Nora's mother is a little—"

"Overbearing," Stuart finished. "And her father is a little—" He frowned, searching for an apt description.

"Overweight?" Ellie offered.

"Just don't let all the glitz and glamour scare you off," Stuart added.

Pete took the invitation from Stuart's hand and smiled. "Thanks. I appreciate the help."

Pete noticed Stuart and Ellie watching until he pulled out of the garage, waving like two proud parents of the prom king as he turned the Mustang down Macondray Lane. Everything had happened so fast, he hadn't had time to think. He'd started the evening with a beer and plans to watch a football game. And here he was, dressed in a monkey suit, on his way to see the woman he loved.

What the hell would he say to her? How could he convince her of his feelings? Rather than take a direct route to swanky Sea Cliff, Pete turned onto Lombard Street and headed toward the Presidio; the picturesque drive would give him time to work out a strategy.

The sun was just beginning to touch the horizon, throwing the verdant landscape into a soft golden light. He followed Lincoln Boulevard, winding past the old parade grounds and the military cemetery, remnants of the time when the Presidio was an active military base. The Golden Gate Bridge rose from the horizon, its top pillars hidden in a thin fog, and he stared at it, tempted to keep right on driving across the Bay.

Though he'd done nothing but think of Nora for the past week, he wasn't sure he was ready to see her yet. Questions about her true feelings for him had plagued his every waking hour. He was certain he loved her, but she'd done nothing but reject him at every turn. With any other woman, he would have walked away long ago, grateful to be free of such stifling emotions and frustrating manipulation. But as long as he believed they had a future together, he couldn't give up. Though she'd never said the words, he'd seen it in her eyes, felt it when she touched him and when she cried out his name in the midst of passion.

By the time Pete passed Baker Beach, he was convinced that seeing Nora tonight was all he really wanted. He snatched up the invitation, searching for the address. He turned west at the edge of the Presidio, away from the pretty little stucco houses of Richmond District and into a whole different world. Sea Cliff couldn't be called a "neighborhood," for the word was much too commonplace for its inhabitants and the grand mansions perched high above the Bay. He assumed Sea Cliff Avenue would be along the water, and within minutes had found the address and turned into the driveway.

He slowed the car and stared at the elegant stone mansion. "Aw, hell," he muttered. He knew Nora came from a wealthy family, but this was more than he'd ever imagined. She was a damn princess! Suddenly, he realized why she had rejected him. No way would her family approve of a match between San Francisco nobility and some ex-jock from a working-class neighborhood in Philly.

A valet jogged to the car and rapped on the window. "Going to the party?" he asked.

Pete shook his head, then drove on. But at the last second, he pulled to a stop and stepped from the car. What did he have to lose? Wasn't Nora worth a few bruises to his ego and some questions about his breeding? In all the time he'd known her, she'd never put on airs. What made him think she'd do so now?

He strode up the driveway and tossed his keys to the valet as he passed. When he reached the elegant front door, he ran his finger under his collar, then tugged at the front of his jacket. He felt as if he were back in the game, standing at the plate, facing a 2–3 count, with runners on base in the bottom of the ninth. Choices had to be made, and he'd have only a split second to make them. "They're no different than me," he murmured. "They put their pants on one leg at a time. Just remember that."

Drawing a deep breath, he walked through the double doors and into an immense foyer of marble and dark wood. Before him, a grand staircase rose to the second floor. Oil paintings decorated the walls, relieved only by small marble busts set in carved wood alcoves. A servant, dressed in tails and a white waistcoat, nodded at him. "Your name, sir?"

"Beckett," he said, handing him the invitation. "Pete Beckett."

The elderly man glanced at the invitation. "This invitation is for Miss Nora and her guest," he said.

"I'm her guest," Pete replied.

The butler frowned. "I've been told that her guest is a Mr. Stuart Anderson. You said your name was Beckett?"

Pete nodded impatiently. Every portrait seemed to be staring at him, unmasking him as the pretender he was. "I'm here in Stuart's place. He gave me the invitation."

The butler looked down his nose at Pete, even though he was at least six inches shorter. "I'm afraid this isn't some rock concert, sir. An invitation to Mrs. Pierce's dinner party isn't transferable. This is a very exclusive charity event."

Pete felt his temper rise and fought the urge to pick up the annoying little man and toss him out onto the front lawn. "I understand. But Nora gave me this invitation and specifically told me to come." The lie sounded convincing. And if the butler decided to find Nora and check it out, Pete would slip into the party unseen. "She'll be very angry if she finds out you refused to let me in. Why don't you go check with her?"

The man thought this over for a moment, then forced a smile. "If you'll just wait here, sir."

While he waited, Pete wandered around the foyer,

examining the paintings. From what he could tell, the Pierce family had been in San Francisco for a long time, since the gold rush days of the mid-1800s. A large painting of a huge old San Francisco mansion drew his attention, and he read that the mansion had been destroyed during the 1906 earthquake. He turned to observe the opposite wall, then froze.

Staring back at him was a likeness of Nora, so exact, so beautiful, that it took his breath away. With a patrician tilt to her head and a slight smile, she watched him with eyes the color of the sky. Her pale hair was loose, falling to her shoulders in soft waves. Desire warmed his blood, and he reached out to the canvas, certain that her skin would feel warm.

"Please don't touch that!"

He yanked his hand away, then turned to find a beautiful woman standing behind him. Though she had a harder edge to her profile, the eyes were the same sapphire shade as Nora's, and the nose, so perfectly straight, could have been the same one he'd kissed countless times.

"Mr. Beckett? I'm Celeste Pierce. I'm afraid there's been some mix-up," she said. "We were expecting Stuart Anderson."

"I know. But I'm a friend of Nora's. If you'll just let me—"

A soft gasp slipped from her perfectly painted lips. "You're the one!" she said, her gaze shrewd and intent. "In the paper. You're the one who—" She didn't finish the accusation.

Pete wondered how much she actually knew. She knew he was the one who got Nora out of jail. But did she realize he was also the one who picked up Nora in a bar? Or did she know he was the one who'd taken her daughter to bed and made her moan with pleasure?

"I think you should leave," Celeste demanded. "Nora is quite occupied with another gentleman right now, and I don't want to disturb her. I'm not sure she'd have any time to talk to you."

Pete met her indifferent gaze with one of his own. He'd faced his share of cool customers, but they'd all had their weaknesses. "How much?" he asked, reaching into his jacket to pull out his checkbook.

Her eyebrow arched, and she sniffed disdainfully. "How much?"

"This is a charity benefit for the opera company, right? How much will it take for me to buy my way in? A thousand, two thousand?"

Though Celeste Pierce had her scruples, when it came to her favorite charities, she also had her price. At three thousand, she nodded imperceptibly. Pete scribbled out a check and held it out to her. "It's for five thousand," he said, trying to forget the fact that he'd just blown his life savings. But Nora was worth it. "The extra two is for a seat next to Nora at the dinner table. I'm sure you can arrange that, can't you?"

She nodded her head just once, then held up her hand to summon the butler. "Courtland, will you see to it that Mr. Beckett is seated next to Nora at dinner?"

The butler bowed, then disappeared into the depths of the house.

"Just follow the hall all the way to the rear of the house," Celeste murmured to Pete. "You'll find Nora on the terrace. I can't guarantee that she'll be happy to see you, but thank you for the check, anyway."

As Pete strolled along the wide hallway, he grinned. He'd gotten past Celeste. Though it had cost him five thousand dollars, it was worth it. Just one look at Nora's portrait had made him desperate to see her. French doors on the far side of the house were thrown open to the night air, and as Pete stepped through them, he had to stop to take in the view.

The mansion was set on a cliff high above the sea, with a wide terrace that led to the edge of the sheer rock face. Party guests milled about, dressed in designer gowns and tailored tuxes. Waiters plied the crowd with champagne and dainty hors d'oeuvres. On the far end of the terrace, a striped tent sheltered tables lit by candlelight. Pete took a glass of bubbly when it was offered, and found a spot near a stone pillar. Standing in the shadows, he sipped at his drink as he scanned the crowd, looking for Nora.

He spotted her at the edge of the terrace, leaning against the stone railing, deep in conversation with a man. He'd looked past her twice before he'd recognized her. Gone was the usual suit and prissy white blouse. Instead, she wore a form-fitting dress, midnight blue and intricately beaded so it sparkled in the soft light from the lanterns strung overhead. Her shoulders and arms were bare, the smooth expanse of her skin broken only by the tiniest straps.

Her hair, so often pulled back into a severe knot, looked soft and touchable, piled on top of her head in a mass of curls. She brushed an errant curl from her face, and his fingers clenched as he imagined himself doing the same, pulling the pins out one by one until he could run his fingers through the soft tresses.

He longed to touch her, to run his hands over her warm skin, to trace a path of kisses from her ear to the sweet curve of her naked shoulder. Pete sucked in the cool evening air and tried to clear his head. He turned his attention to her companion and felt a prick of jealousy, especially after noting the rapt expression on the guy's face.

Pete gulped down the last of his champagne, then grabbed a fresh glass from a passing waiter. As he watched Nora, he mulled over what he wanted to say to her. But he hadn't a clue how she might react when she saw him. Would she be happy to see him?

As he watched her, he came to realize that she wasn't enjoying the discussion. Every now and then, her companion made to touch her, and she deftly avoided his hand. On closer inspection, Pete could see her smile was forced and her demeanor stiff and formal. She definitely looked like a woman who needed rescuing.

Pete smiled to himself. He was just the man for the job.

"LASER TECHNOLOGY is changing the whole face of modern surgery. We haven't seen medical progress like this since the introduction of antibiotics!"

Nora forced a smile, then nodded. Good Lord, if she had to listen to one more boring blow-by-blow account of one more disgusting surgical procedure, she'd scream. She glanced over her shoulder, tapping her foot impatiently. Where was Stuart? He'd promised to meet her at the house ten minutes before the party started. He was already an hour late.

"I'd love to have you come to the hospital and watch a surgery."

Nora snapped her attention back to Elliott Alexander. *Dr.* Elliott Alexander. He'd spent the last half hour glued to her side, and no matter how bored she appeared, he seemed to delight in regaling her with yet another tale of his medical prowess. "I don't think so," she said, trying to appear grateful for the invitation. "I'm rather squeamish at the sight of blood."

"But that's the wonderful thing about laser surgery. There's very little blood."

Nora scrambled to find an alternative subject. Or a polite way to extricate herself from the unending conversation. She glanced over to the tent to see the waiters preparing the tables for the first course. If her mother's party followed the usual schedule, Nora had precisely five minutes to race to the tables and rearrange the place cards so that Elliott was sitting on the other end of the tent, rather than next to her.

She had come to the party reluctantly, but willing to socialize for her mother's sake. And she had to admit that it felt good to put on makeup and a brand-new gown. Strangely, no one had seemed interested in her recent scandalous behavior. Buffy Sinclair's husband had been caught in bed with his wife's hairstylist, and that juicy news had far surpassed Nora's measly arrest.

Still, every minute she spent with the very eligible Elliott made her wish all the more that she were sitting behind home plate at a Giants' game with Pete Beckett, munching on a chili dog and burping from warm beer. Or strolling the streets on Telegraph Hill. Nora sighed softly. Or rolling around on his bed in a tangle of sheets and limbs.

It wasn't until she saw how incompatible she was with Elliott that she truly realized what she and Pete had shared. There was an invisible connection between them, an unbreakable thread woven out of passion and affection and respect, a connection she'd stretched so far that it threatened to break.

Though Pete had the capacity to turn her into a blithering idiot or a sex-starved wanton, he also made her feel safe—and cherished. A tremor shook her body as she thought about the exquisite feel of his body stretched over the length of hers, the flood of sensation she had experienced when he came inside her, the pure ecstasy they'd shared. She had never felt so loved, so needed.

But where did passion end and true emotion begin? She'd only had a handful of lovers in her life, and not one had swept her away with desire as Pete had. When she was with him, she couldn't think straight. Her common sense and pragmatic nature seemed to dissolve beneath his touch. As Prudence Trueheart, she'd always had all the answers. But why couldn't she come up with any answers for herself?

As she listened to Elliott drone on about new anesthetic techniques, she allowed her mind to drift. A lazy replay of that last night with Pete flickered in her head, like some erotic movie. She had never thought herself uninhibited when it came to sex, but she hadn't been able to hold back. The chill night air cooled her warm cheeks, and she drew a deep breath, the salt tang clearing her head and bringing the images into sharper focus....

"Ladies and gentlemen, dinner is served."

Yanked out of her daydream by Courtland's pronouncement, Nora brushed aside thoughts of Pete and quickly excused herself, determined to alter the seating arrangements. She hurried toward the tent, but Elliott was more tenacious than she had expected. He followed close behind and found their cards near the head of the first table before she did.

"Here you are," he said, as the guests began to take their places.

Groaning inwardly, Nora allowed him to pull out her chair. She snatched the napkin from her plate and spread it across her lap, as Elliott sat to her left. The chair to the right of her remained empty until nearly everyone was seated. Elliott had engaged her in yet another medical adventure, when the gentleman sat down beside her. She turned to greet him politely, but her introduction died in her throat.

"Wha—what are you doing here?" Nora could barely believe her eyes. It was as if her hazy fantasies had suddenly sprung to life, in living color. Only in this dream, Pete wasn't naked. He was fully dressed in a tux, the starched shirt setting off his deeply tanned skin, the fit emphasizing his broad shoulders and narrow waist.

He leaned closer and whispered in her ear, his breath like a caress on her face. "I heard there was an alfresco dinner going on and I wanted to use all that good etiquette you taught me."

Pete drew back and reached across her plate, offering his hand to Elliott Alexander. "Hi. I'm Pete Beckett. I'm a friend of Nora's. Actually, I'm Nora's date."

"You are not!" she cried.

Pete chuckled. "Well, that's true. I'm more than just a date. I'm her—"

"Co-worker," she interrupted. "*Ex* co-worker, to be precise."

Elliott hesitantly took Pete's hand. "Elliott Alexander, M.D. Are you Pete Beckett, the sports columnist for the *Herald?*"

Pete nodded and spread his napkin on his lap. "That's me."

Elliott looked impressed as he grasped for words. "Gee, I read your column every day. I loved the one you did on free agency."

"Yeah, I got a lot of mail on that one. What did you think about the one on Candlestick?"

Elliott nodded and grinned. "A classic. I remember seeing you play. You were a great glove man."

Nora's neck was getting stiff from following the conversation. "Would you two like to sit next to each other?" she asked. "In fact, if you like, I can just eat in the kitchen."

Pete put his arm around her shoulders. "Darling, why would we want to do that?" He let his gaze drift down to her bare shoulders. "Have I told you how beautiful you look tonight? That dress is...incredible. Don't you think Nora looks beautiful tonight, Elliott?"

Nora tried to ignore the compliment, but the fact that he'd noticed her appearance sent a tiny thrill racing through her. He didn't look so bad himself. He had a body meant for a tux. Her gaze drifted down to the onyx studs, and she imagined herself working them open, one by one, parting the pleated front of his shirt so she could kiss his smooth chest. She swallowed hard. This was exactly what she'd been fighting so hard against, this knack he had for stirring her fire.

"You look very nice, too," she murmured.

The waiters worked their way down the tables, serving the first course and pouring wine. Nora picked up her goblet and nervously spun it around between her fingers. "How did you even get in?" she asked, turning so Elliott wouldn't overhear.

Pete grinned. "Stuart gave me his invitation. He and Ellie showed up at my apartment a few hours ago. It seems Stuart had a previous engagement, and they didn't want to leave you here alone…and dateless. Although I noticed Elliott was keeping you company."

Jealousy dripped from his offhand comment, and once again Nora felt her resolve slipping away. "And where did you get the tux?"

"From my closet," he said. "When you go to as many award banquets as I do, it's a sound investment. As was the donation I made to the San Francisco Opera. Your mother was quite pleased. I think she likes me, and my bank account."

"How much did she hit you up for?" Nora asked.

Pete waited as his wineglass was filled, then picked it up and took a sip. "Five thousand. But that included a seat next to you at dinner."

Her eyes went wide, and she coughed. Grabbing her water goblet, she took a long drink, then set it down with a clatter. "Y-you gave my mother five thousand dollars just to sit next to me? But this dinner is only a thousand dollars a plate."

Pete shrugged. "Then, I'll just have to eat five meals, won't I? Or get my money's worth in some other way."

Nora shoved her chair back and stood up. "Elliott, would you excuse us, please?" She grabbed Pete's arm and dragged him from his chair. "I need to check on something for my mother." Pete carefully folded his napkin and set it beside his plate. Then he followed her at an easy pace. When they'd reached the privacy of the house, she let go of his arm and cursed softly.

"What are you doing here?" she demanded.

He pulled her into the shadow of an alcove and spread his hands around her waist, tugging her closer. "You do look beautiful tonight. When I saw you in that dress, I felt like I'd been hit by a bus. God, I've missed you." He nuzzled her hair. "I've missed us."

Nora pushed his hands away. Sweet talk was not going to lighten her mood. "You can't just burst in unannounced! And whatever possessed you to give my mother five thousand dollars?"

He stepped back, and his gaze drifted down the length of her body, a tiny smile of appreciation quirking his lips. Suddenly, she felt naked, as if he could see right through the beads and the filmy fabric. "It was worth it to see you in that dress," he murmured.

She sighed and took a deep breath. "Stop saying things like that!"

"Why?" Pete asked. "Are you afraid of the truth, Nora? You've been avoiding it for so long, no wonder it frightens you."

"I don't know what the truth is. Not when it comes to...us."

"Well, Nora, here's a truth. I've missed you this past week. I've tried to forget you, but I've learned that I can't be happy unless I see your face every morning and every night and a hundred times in between. Dreaming about you just isn't enough."

Every good intention suddenly seeped out of her body, and she felt lost, vulnerable, unable to resist any longer. "Pete, please don't—"

He reached up and pressed his warm palm to her cheek. "You wanted the truth? Here's another truth. I've never felt this way before. I don't know how I know, but I do know. I'm in love with you, Nora, and it's not going to go away just because you want it to."

"You're not in love with me," she said, holding her finger up to his lips to stop his words. "You're in love with a fantasy, a woman who doesn't exist." He stared down at her, and though he didn't speak, his eyes continued to profess his feelings. She wanted to throw herself into his arms, to finally accept that they were meant to be together. But something was holding her back.

"She does exist," he finally said. "And I can prove it." He grabbed her arm and dragged her farther into the house, throwing doors open and glancing inside empty rooms and dark closets. When he reached the powder room under the stairs, he steered Nora inside and slammed the door behind them both.

"You want proof? I'll give you proof." He swept her into his arms and brought his mouth down on hers, kissing her so deeply and thoroughly that she couldn't draw a decent breath. Nora's head spun; her body tingled, every nerve on edge, vibrating with anticipation. Sweet sensation flooded her, and she felt weak, defenseless.

She'd dreamed of this moment, these wonderful feelings that he brought forth with his touch—the warmth, the ache, the pure need that couldn't be satisfied with simple fantasy.

"Tell me what you want," he murmured, his voice hot and urgent, his lips pressed against her neck.

Nora's fingers moved to the onyx studs, and without thinking, she began to work them open. It was as if an unseen force were driving her, making her body move without conscious command. When the last stud fell to the marble floor, she pushed his shirt aside and pressed her lips to his warm skin. His heart beat, strong and even, beneath her palm, the rhythm drawing her away from the real world, from all her doubts and insecurities.

This was what she wanted, this man so strong and

self-assured, his touch so gentle and stirring. These feelings rushing through her body and clouding her mind. This was all she ever wanted and all she ever needed. "I want you," Nora murmured, her voice raw and breathless.

"Here?" he asked. "Now?"

She nodded, pressing her lips along the ridge of his collarbone, tracing a path to the notch at the base of his neck. His thumb hooked under her chin, and he forced Nora's eyes to meet his. She looked up at him through a haze of passion to find him smiling.

"I rest my case," he said, before he brushed his mouth across hers.

"What?"

"I think that's all the proof you need, sweetheart. You were willing to make love to me here, in your mother's powder room, in the middle of your mother's party. I think it's time you admit that you *are* that woman. The woman in the dark wig."

Nora blinked, trying to focus her thoughts on his statement. She glanced down at her dress, and then spun around to look at her reflection in the mirror. Her face was flushed and her lips damp from his kisses, but there was no doubt. She was staring at Nora Pierce and no one else. "It was me," she said, drawing her fingertips over her warm cheeks. "I am her."

Pete stepped up behind her, wrapping his arms around her waist and resting his chin on her shoulder. "You always have been. You just didn't want to admit it." He gently turned her in his arms and took her face between his hands. "I know we didn't start this the right way," he said softly, gazing intently into her eyes. "But we can go back to the beginning. We'll take things nice and slow. We'll have a few dates and then maybe I'll kiss you." He brushed his lips against hers again, then chuckled softly. "See, that wasn't so bad, was it?"

Nora felt another blush warm her cheeks as her gaze dropped to his naked chest. "It's going to be awfully hard to start at the beginning, don't you think?" she asked, tracing a finger along the soft dusting of hair from his collarbone to his belt.

"I suppose we could be a little more intimate, since we aren't exactly strangers." His mouth drifted down her neck to her bare shoulder. "And when the time is right, I'll make slow, delicious love to you." He tipped her back against the edge of the pedestal sink, his hands spanning her waist as his mouth found her earlobe. "And maybe, sometime next month, you and I can get married."

Nora gasped as his kisses sent sweet pleasure shooting through her—and then his words registered. "Married?"

"We'll have a beautiful wedding and an exhausting honeymoon. And after a time, we'll start a family and—"

"Wait!" Nora cried, pulling out of his embrace. "I'm still stuck on the wedding part."

"I know I can't turn back time," Pete said, his voice anxious, "but I talked to Arthur Sterling yesterday. My contract with his syndicate is up at the end of the year. I told him if he didn't hire you back, I wasn't going to sign another contract with him. I can make this right for you, Nora."

"I don't want my job back," she said. "Getting fired was the best thing that ever happened to me. Or maybe the second-best thing." She drew a deep breath. "Ask me again."

He frowned. "What? I didn't do the proposal right?" Pete sighed dramatically, then dropped to one knee on the bathroom floor. "Nora Pierce, I love you now and I plan to love you for the rest of your life and beyond. Marry me—"

"Oh, my God!"

Celeste stood in the doorway, outrage suffusing her features. Pete looked over his shoulder but didn't bother to rise; he held Nora's fingers in his.

"What are you two doing in here?" Celeste glanced down at Pete, then held out her hand as though to ward off the sight. "No, no. Don't tell me. Oh, I can't bear this. I simply can't. This, on top of my opera party. It's just too much."

Nora sent Pete a winsome smile, then pulled him to his feet. "Don't worry, Mother. I'll make sure you don't have to do any planning for the wedding."

Celeste's apoplectic expression suddenly disappeared as her gaze jumped between Pete and Nora. "Don't be ridiculous. No daughter of mine is going to plan her own wedding. That's *my* job." Her hands fluttered, and finally, unable to contain herself any longer, she gave Nora a quick peck on the cheek. "We'll have to talk about this later. The soup is cold and the wine is not up to snuff." Celeste gave Pete the once over, then sighed. "I suppose you'll have to do." With that, she turned on her heel and hurried off.

"Wait until the day we tell her she's going to be a grandmother," Nora murmured. "She may decide to jump off the Bay Bridge."

Pete pulled her against his body and pressed his forehead to hers. "Children—I like the sound of that.

You know," he said, reaching over her shoulder to shut the bathroom door, "we could make our excuses and get started on that right away."

Nora pushed up on her toes and brushed a tempting kiss across his lips. "I'm not ready to share you right now. I want to keep you all to myself."

Pete's arms snaked around her waist and he picked her up and twirled her around and around in the tiny room until she was breathless. "All right," he said. "It's a deal. But you have to promise me that you'll wear the wig at least once or twice a week."

Nora tipped her head back and giggled, then gazed down into her lover's eyes. "I've never been able to refuse you," she said. "And I'm not going to start now."

Epilogue

VIC'S WAS CROWDED with Monday night football fans. All the televisions were tuned to the Niners game, and at every offensive play, a rousing cheer rattled the bottles lining the back of the bar. Pete watched the game without much interest. He'd stopped at Vic's after work for lack of anything else to do. Nora had been out of town for the past two days on business, and the commotion here was much easier to take than the silence of an empty house.

She'd refused his offer of help at the *Herald* and had struck out on her own, prepared to enter graduate school at UC Berkeley. But she'd underestimated the visibility and the popularity of Prudence Trueheart. Or the reputation Celeste Pierce had as a fund-raiser. When Nora had applied for a docent position at the San Francisco Museum of Modern Art, they'd offered her a full-time job in their marketing department. And Celeste had immediately shifted her loyalties from the opera company to the museum.

Though Pete was proud of all Nora had accomplished, he still couldn't help missing her when she went out of town once or twice a month. This time, it was New York, and work on the brochure for a new Chagall exhibit due to show at the museum before the end of the year. She'd be back tomorrow morning, and he planned to take the day off work to give her a proper welcome.

He picked up his mug and took a slow sip of his beer, then tried again to focus on the game. But when the guy next to him left, a woman stepped up to the bar and slid onto the empty stool. The scent of perfume wafted through the smoky air, and Pete recognized it immediately.

He wasn't even tempted to glance at her. Though she smelled like Nora, she wasn't Nora. And it had been months since he'd even thought about another woman. Though he'd never have thought it possible, Pete had become a one-woman man, and Nora had become the center of his life.

"Who's winning?"

Pete blinked, then slowly turned to look at the woman sitting beside him. She wore a bright green dress with a low-cut neck, the perfect color to set off her long auburn hair. A slow smile curled his lips as he gazed into sapphire-blue eyes, the color of the sky above the Pacific. He fought the urge to pull her into his arms and kiss her senseless. Instead, he decided to play along with her little game.

"I haven't been watching," he said, letting his gaze drift over her face. "Can I buy you a drink?"

She pursed her lips in a pretty little pout as she considered his offer, then shook her head. "I'm not here for the drinks."

He felt her hand slide along his thigh, then slowly move between his legs. Desire twisted at his core, and he grew hard beneath the gentle pressure of her fingers. He glanced over his shoulder at the door, wondering how he'd get out without the entire bar noticing the state of his arousal. "What are you here for?"

"You," she said, placing a soft kiss on his cheek.

Pete chuckled. "I wasn't expecting you. Why are you here?"

Her lips drifted down to his jaw. "I was lonely. I needed a man. I needed...you."

He wrapped his arm around her shoulders and gently fingered the wig. "I like the color," he said. "And the dress—well, it's very nice. Maybe I can help you take it off?"

She drew back and gave him a seductive smile. "Here? There's a dark little spot back in the corner. No one will see us."

Pete growled, then pulled her off the bar stool and kissed her. "If you know what's good for you, you'll come home with me right now—before I embarrass both of us."

She shrugged, then pushed away from the bar and began a sultry walk to the door, her hips swaying provocatively. Pete grabbed his jacket and held it in front of him as he followed her, smiling to himself.

It was hard to believe Nora could ever have thought herself anything but exciting.

MILLS & BOON®

Makes any time special™

Mills & Boon publish 29 new titles every month. Select from...

Modern Romance™   Tender Romance™

Sensual Romance™

Medical Romance™ Historical Romance™

MAT2

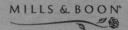

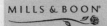

2 BOOKS
AND A SURPRISE GIFT!

We would like to take this opportunity to thank you for reading this Mills & Boon® book by offering you the chance to take TWO more specially selected titles from the Sensual Romance™ series absolutely FREE! We're also making this offer to introduce you to the benefits of the Reader Service™—

★ FREE home delivery
★ FREE monthly Newsletter
★ FREE gifts and competitions
★ Exclusive Reader Service discounts
★ Books available before they're in the shops

Accepting these FREE books and gift places you under no obligation to buy; you may cancel at any time, even after receiving your free shipment. Simply complete your details below and return the entire page to the address below. *You don't even need a stamp!*

YES! Please send me 2 free Sensual Romance™ books and a surprise gift. I understand that unless you hear from me, I will receive 4 superb new titles every month for just £2.49 each, postage and packing free. I am under no obligation to purchase any books and may cancel my subscription at any time. The free books and gift will be mine to keep in any case.

T1ZEC

Ms/Mrs/Miss/Mr ....Initials ....
                                                                        BLOCK CAPITALS PLEASE
Surname ....
Address ....

....
....Postcode ....

Send this whole page to:
UK: FREEPOST CN81, Croydon, CR9 3WZ
EIRE: PO Box 4546, Kilcock, County Kildare (stamp required)

Offer valid in UK and Eire only and not available to current Reader Service subscribers to this series. We reserve the right to refuse an application and applicants must be aged 18 years or over. Only one application per household. Terms and prices subject to change without notice. Offer expires 31st December 2001. As a result of this application, you may receive further offers from Harlequin Mills & Boon Limited and other carefully selected companies. If you would prefer not to share in this opportunity please write to The Data Manager at the address above.

Mills & Boon® is a registered trademark owned by Harlequin Mills & Boon Limited.
Sensual Romance™ is a registered trademark used under license.